DROWNED
MAN'S LODE

Also by Robert McCaig

The Burntwood Men
The Rangemaster
Wild Justice

DROWNED MAN'S LODE

ROBERT MCCAIG

CUTTING EDGE

ISBN-13: 978-1-952138-33-1

Published by
Cutting Edge Publishing
PO Box 8212
Calabasas, CA 91372

www.cuttingedgebooks.com

For Freda

CHAPTER ONE

The first knock was hesitant, timid. Kendall, who was half dozing on the bed in undershirt and trousers, raised up on an elbow. The knock came again, sharper, more insistent.

"Just a minute," Kendall called. He got up and grabbed a clean shirt from the bureau drawer. He was ramming the tails inside his belt as he walked on stocking feet to the door. He turned the knob.

A girl thrust her way into the room. Kendall, stepping back, stared at her. He had never seen her before. She pushed the door shut and set her back against it. She was, he saw, blonde, lovely and extremely distrait.

"Your name is Kendall?" she asked.

He nodded, leaving the initiative to the girl.

"You claim to be an engineer, Kendall. You've hired out to superintend the Blue Grouse tunnel job for Mr. Tarow."

Again he took ironic amusement in merely nodding.

She fumbled with the catch of her reticule. She took a piece of paper from the bag. She extended it toward Kendall.

"Then what is the meaning of this?" she demanded.

He took it. By the paper and type, it was from one of the mining journals. The line beneath the halftone cut read "Morley Kendall." It was not a particularly good likeness.

He handed it back to the girl. "What of it?" he asked.

Anger suffused her lovely face. "What of it? This is not a picture of you!"

"Of course not. Big Morley is six-four and weighs close to two thirty. I'm five-ten, and seldom tip the scales at much more than a hundred and sixty pounds."

"So!" There was a note of triumph in her voice. "You admit you're not Morley Kendall. Yet you're brazen enough to palm yourself off as a construction expert to Jason Tarow and Aaron Hagen and the whole town of Juniper."

He frowned. "I'm afraid I don't follow you, miss. My name is Kendall. I'm an engineer, a graduate of Colorado School of Mines. I have a perfectly legitimate tender of employment from Mr. Jason Tarow himself. Just a moment."

He rummaged in the dispatch box that held his personal papers. He brought out a creased and crumpled telegraph form. He handed it to the girl, who took it warily. He watched her as she read it. He knew the wording of it by heart.

JUNIPER MONTANA
MAY THIRD 1896
M KENDALL
CARE BONANZA AND WESTERN RAILROAD
SUTTER CITY CALIFORNIA
   I HAVE HARDROCK TUNNEL JOB ESTIMATED TOTAL COST ONE AND ONE HALF MILLION DOLLARS STOP WILL YOU TAKE IT ON AS SUPERINTENDENT WITH FULL AUTHORITY SALARY ONE THOUSAND PER MONTH PLUS QUARTERS AND EXPENSES STOP ADDED BONUS IF COMPLETED UNDER FOURTEEN MONTHS STOP THIS ONE COULD BE TOUGHER AND MEANER THAN THE RHYOLITE BORE SO I NEED THE KIND OF MAN WHO DROVE THAT ONE STOP WIRE YOUR ACCEPTANCE COLLECT
JASON TAROW

She tossed the telegram disdainfully to the table.

"How did you get this? It was sent to Morley Kendall."

He shrugged. "It was delivered to me, Michael Kendall. I'm a hard-rock man, I worked with my brother on the Rhyolite bore. So I was hired on a misunderstanding. Well, well. Fortunately, I'm competent to handle the job and Mr. Tarow seems quite well pleased with my work to date."

"Because he thinks you're Morley Kendall!" she cried. "And you think you can get away with the impersonation. But no cheap grafter is going to botch up Jason's tunnel. I won't let you."

Her hand came from her open purse. Nickel gleamed in the yellow light of the electric bulb. She was excited, but the gun muzzle she pointed at Kendall was rock steady.

"You, Mr. Michael Kendall, or whatever your name is, will get out of Juniper. Tonight, on the southbound train. If you don't I assure you it will be too bad for you."

Kendall looked at the gun. "I never argue with loaded artillery," he said. "I'll pack my grips. And I'll have to write a note for Tarow."

"Start packing. And you won't need a note. I'll tell him."

He piled things from the bureau into the open suitcases.

"Tell him I found another error in Baumer's original survey. About ten feet over. It will mean adjusting the grade. Tarow will have to run it out, since I won't be here." He stacked clean shirts into the suitcase. He straightened. "By the way, who are you? And why are you so dead set to protect Jason Tarow?"

"I'm Fran Diamond, Mr. Tarow's secretary. We have—well, an understanding. As soon as Blue Grouse is a success..."

"You'll marry the little man, eh? But you want to ensure the success of the tunnel, so you can share his future millions. Mighty wise young lady. No love in a tarpaper shack for you."

Her face was angry. She took an impulsive step toward him.

3

"You boor! I don't care about the money. Blue Grouse is Jason's big dream. If it fails, I don't know what it will do to him. He is *not* a funny little man, Kendall. He has brains and vision and driving force. In twelve years he has come up from engine wiping in the Butte shops of the Utah Northern to a position that has won the respect of the big men of the mining industry. They are trusting him with the millions necessary for Luscon and the Blue Grouse. Will you laugh at that?"

He turned his scarred face toward her. "Why should I laugh at Tarow? I like him. And I was looking forward to building his tunnel for him."

"Blue Grouse isn't a job for any run-of-the-mill mucker, Kendall," she said, still angry. "So, since you aren't Morley Kendall, we don't want you in Juniper. I'm going to ..."

The gun wavered. With the speed of a stooping hawk, Kendall's hand seized her wrist. He twisted brutally, careless of hurting her. The girl cried out. The gun fell, thudding on the worn carpet. He kicked it under the bed. She tried to scratch his eyes. He twisted his head away and pinned her hands in a tight vise that pulled her up close to him, her eyes blazing. She was nearly as tall as Kendall.

She wrenched one hand free and slammed Kendall across the face. The blow brought a stab of pain to his eyes. He drove forward, thrusting his weight. The edge of the bed caught the girl at the knees and she fell backward, Kendall with her. He felt the taut, lithe curves of her body beneath him. Like a lean tiger cat, he thought.

She fought furiously. It took a surge of strength to spread-eagle her arms across the bed. She kicked at him, arching her back in a bridge. He brought a leg across her knees, forcing her back onto the coverlet. Panting, she subsided, but her eyes still blazed. Still holding her arms, he raised himself, looking at her.

That stormy face, the challenge of the red lips so close to his, were more than Kendall could forego. He kissed her. She tried to bite him, her lips twisting beneath his. Then the resistance went out of her. For a brief instant, she returned his kiss. He held the fierce sweetness of it for a long moment. Then, thrusting back the urgency that was stirring in him, he lifted his weight from her and stood up.

She lay there without moving, as if gathering her resources. Contempt in her eyes, she did not even reach to straighten the skirt and petticoats which had twisted high on her lovely legs. Then she came up in one swift motion, without warning, diving for the gun. He reached it first and shoved her back onto the bed.

He shucked the five cartridges out of the little revolver and dropped them into his pocket. He reversed the gun and handed it to her. She dropped it into her purse and flung the purse on the table. She sat up on the edge of the bed, smoothing down her skirts. She watched him, beaten but unconquered.

Kendall dropped into the rocker and grinned at her.

"A truce, Miss Diamond?" he asked. "I admire a fighter, even a losing one. God knows, I've had my own defeats. Blue Grouse may yet be one of them, through no fault of mine. But I don't intend it so. How about listening to my side of this?"

"Go ahead," she said tersely.

Mike Kendall had learned to keep his dreams and hopes and disappointments to himself. But now he had a desperate urge to tell Fran Diamond all the things that had been bottled up within him for so long a time. Only in the ultimate clock-tick of time did prudence stop him. But she deserved the truth as far as he could reveal it.

"Miss Diamond, Morley Kendall is my brother. He is one of the big wheels in western construction, and for good reason. He has built bridges and tunnels and railroads that lesser men called impossible. And for ten years I've worked with Big Morley— worked as crew chief and rigger foreman and night super. Morley is the best, but I am a good man too, by God! I can build this double-damned tunnel of Jason Tarow's, build it right. Maybe even beat the estimate, with the help of the good Lord. And don't you forget it, even Big Morley depends on His help too."

"You have a good opinion of yourself," the girl said.

"And why not? I'm this sure of it—I don't much care what you tell Jason Tarow. The man's smart. If he fires me, he might lose a full year on the tunnel, hunting a replacement superintendent. I think he'll decide I can cut 'er."

"You had it all figured out, didn't you? You must want this job badly, Kendall, to batten on your brother's reputation to get it. Why?"

He spread his hands. "The money, of course," he told her, trying to make the explanation ring true. Then he came perilously close to the truth, knowing he might be giving the girl a stick to beat him with. "Besides, when I bring in Blue Grouse, men may speak of Mike Kendall in the same breath with Big Morley."

The girl looked at him, frowning. She stood up, brushing her skirts down. Picking up her reticule, she walked to the door. With one hand on the knob, she looked at Kendall.

"All right," she said. "Every man deserves his chance. I won't say anything to Jason. But so help me, Kendall, at the first sign that you are booting the Blue Grouse job, I'll be ready. I'll get even with you for any damage to Jason, as sure as God made little apples." She opened the door. "And as for the kiss, keep it. It's the last you'll ever get."

Long after the door closed, Kendall did not move. Then he lit a cigar. She's no tame kitten, he thought. Wonder if the little man knows what a handful he's getting in this Fran Diamond. But, he thought, handful or not, hers is the kind of loyalty that can't be bought. He was remembering, with grim distaste, the lesson of Liz McKey, who had sold out her loyalty to him as cheaply as she had her magnificent body to Big Morley. He had been younger then, and a fool, as Morley had pointed out with his big, booming laugh. But it had hurt. Even now the memory intruded into his relations with women.

No use pretending he didn't envy Morley. He did. It was always Big Morley in the midst of the brass when the last spike was driven or the ribbon cut; Morley who had his pictures in the paper, the casual offer of half a dozen new big jobs whenever he finished one. And it was Mike behind the scenes, keeping the shaky cut from sliding, arranging the big show blast, getting the special train there on time while keeping the filthy construction stiffs, the ragtag and bobtail, out of sight of the moneyed gentlemen in the high starched collars. Now Mike had a good job of his own.

Morley had handed it to him on a platter, of course. Tossed him the telegram just as he had boarded a train for the East. What did Morley care for Blue Grouse when he was off across the seas for an audience with the Tsar of All the Russias? The kid brother could handle Blue Grouse, while Morley dug a tunnel under the Urals, bridged the mighty Volga, shaped a canal to the Baltic for the Tsar. America already knew Big Morley. Now it would be the world.

Easy enough. A fine big gesture, worthy of the legendary Morley Kendall, but ignoring the fact that for ten years Mike Kendall had been hidden in the big man's shadow, and that for six of those years, there had lurked the terrible memory of the Lobchick tunnel, and the three men who had died there. No fault of Mike Kendall's, but even now the panic rose in him, the illogical horror of underground water. It had come so suddenly, when he and Plato Gill and Raftery and the other man—Kollada?—were inspecting a heavy water seepage at the working face of Lobchick. Plato Gill had struck twice with his pick and the face had split open like the springing of a trap, gushing forth a stream of water as thick as a man's body that struck them all with tremendous pressure, hurling them against the walls and piling up in seconds to a rushing river in the low ground ahead of the face. Then Big Morley had come, thrusting through surging water as deep as his barrel chest. Somehow he had brought Mike out. But the others were gone.

His hand went now to the three wales embossed down one cheek: the visible scars of Lobchick. But there were deeper ones, which no one could see but himself. The dread of wild water, the fear of making decisions that might mean a job. Right now he felt again the cold sweat breaking out on his forehead. He had no business with Blue Grouse. There was almost a certainty of underground water. In fact the purpose of the tunnel was to tap and drain the Castle Lode. It was a big job. too big for a man afraid, a man twisted by memory and broken confidence. Fran Diamond had given him an out. Why didn't he take it before he made some error that brought injury or death to other good men?

But even as the sick fear rose in him. he knew he would keep on at Blue Grouse. The decision had been made back in Sutter City, when Kendall had wrestled with the pros and cons in the desperate hours of the night. He had dumped his chips in the middle of the table, win, lose or draw, with never a Big Morley Kendall to cry to for help. It must be now. he thought, or I'm finished. I'll find out if I'm an engineer, or a skid-road bum.

And. as the clincher, he couldn't let Jason Tarow down. As Kendall had told Fran Diamond, he liked the little man. Tarow was a natural butt of fortune, a born target of fate. Sharpers and con men found him unerringly, to weave around him the web of their tawdry schemes. But somehow the little man came out on top, each time with a few dollars more. Now this stake was sunk in the Luscon Syndicate, which held title to the drowned-out workings of the Winkin Jack mine. Tarow had drawn some big fortunes into Luscon. Then he had talked the brass, along with Aaron Hagen, the owner of the Case Ace, into Blue Grouse, into tossing a million and a half into a tunnel to drain the Castle Lode.

Kendall shook his head. The little man was a promoter to inspire awe. Only Phil van Zandt, of all the Juniper mineowners, had refused his support. Not only that, Tarow had told Kendall, van Zandt was bucking the plan at every turn. Kendall supposed that since the Queen o' Hearts had not broken into the underground stream, van Zandt felt secure in his production. He was the kind who wanted always to be the king of the hill. A dangerous man, Kendall thought. Ruthless, arrogant and with the money to buy anything.

He looked at his watch and jumped up. In less than an hour he would be guest of honor at a dinner at the Hagen's. He pushed his black thoughts aside. As he shaved, he thought, "Maybe Morley *is* dining with the Tsar. But I'm the big frog in this puddle!"

CHAPTER TWO

Kendall toyed with the inhaler of Courvoisier, brushing circles in the snowy linen of the table. He was tired. Replete with food and wine, he merely drifted in the murmur of conversation. He half heard the argument going on between Dooley Swain, editor of Juniper's weekly, *The Prospector,* and Von Bulow, the bearded doctor. He caught the words "Bryan" and "free silver" and thought idly they must be fighting words in this gold-mining community. Juniper was of the opinion that the silver panic of 1893 was just the comeuppance the silver upstarts deserved.

"You, Kendall," a heavy voice challenged beside him. "You think you're the man who is going to lick Castle Mountain?"

Kendall turned. This was Phil van Zandt, the owner of the Queen o' Hearts. He had a tall glass in his hand. His jowly face was flushed, and a gleam of perspiration shone on his upper lip. Disregarding the upholstery, he put a foot on the chair beside Kendall, leaning a forearm on the back of it.

"I don't think you're the man to do it," he went on.

Kendall sipped the golden brandy. "That so?" he asked.

"Oh, you've got a big reputation, Kendall. But you're not going to fatten it by tapping the Castle Lode. This is one time you'll run for home with your tail between your legs."

The man's tone rasped at Kendall. He curbed his anger. He said mildly, "I didn't know the job was that tough."

"The job is tough enough. But more than that, I don't intend to have so-called engineers digging and blasting in the guts of that mountain. I want well enough left alone."

"That's between you, Tarow, and Hagen," Kendall said. "I'm just a hired hand. And I don't scare worth a damn, van Zandt."

The mineowner banged the flat of his hand on the table. The glasses jumped. Kendall saw Hagen cast an inquiring glance toward them.

"They had better listen to me, and so had you, mister. I've told them over and over that if they disturb the rock strata, open up some new vein in that sponge of rock, they may drown out the Queen. They claim to be draining their mines. Well, I'm not going to stand still for them drowning me out, like a gopher in a hole."

"You don't know much about rock, do you, van Zandt? Nor about men, either?" Kendall asked.

"I can hire clowns like you for the rock, and I can handle the men myself, no matter how hard and tough they come," the mineowner said. "I think, Kendall, you had better get out of town. Damn' sudden, too. I might even give you some small change to help you on your way."

Kendall laughed. "Come off it, van Zandt. You're not talking to a kid now. I made a bargain with Tarow. I'm sticking with it."

"You're a stupid blockhead!" van Zandt growled. Abruptly he turned away. He walked to the window, putting his glass on the sill. Staring out into the darkness, he scratched a match and lit a cigar, taking great pains to get it burning evenly. Finally he dropped the spent match hissing into his glass and walked away, leaving the glass.

Turning back to the table, Kendall caught Aaron Hagen's unspoken question. He shook his head. Hagen grinned, made a gesture with the long, unlighted perfecto in his hand, and went back to his conversation with Tarow. Kendall watched him, liking the man. He respected the strong honest face, the scarred hands. Only a few short years ago this man had been swinging a single jack in a coyote hole beyond the Neversweat. Now he was at home in this room of silver and lace and crystal. Yet Kendall had the feeling that if the turn of fortune put the single jack back in Hagen's hand, he would swing it well and cheerfully.

The ladies had gone into the parlor some time ago, but Hagen and his men guests seemed in no hurry to finish their brandy and their cigars. Kendall flicked open his hunting-case watch. Eight thirty. He felt a slight impatience. Men he worked with all the time, but seldom did he have a chance to enjoy the company of charming women. His interest, he admitted, centered in his companion at dinner, Ruth Hagen. She was attractive, with her dark hair and fine eyes, her animation of speech and action. She had shown a penetrating insight into the foibles of the inhabitants of Juniper, of high or low degree. Nor had the girl been repelled by his scarred face. Some women were.

Restless, he stood up and went over to the tall windows. Looking out, he sipped the Courvoisier, rolling its fragrant mellowness over his tongue. The Hagens' great gingerbread mansion was high on a slope above the town of Juniper. Below it blinked the lights of the miners' homes, and, farther still, the mercantile places of Gold Street made solid blocks of light. Five of the main street intersections had the new electric arc lights. The town was more up-to-date, Kendall realized, than most of its eastern counterparts.

Across the valley more arc lights sputtered blue against the hill. They lit up the gaunt gallows-frame of the Queen o' Hearts, and nearer, the hoist of the Case Ace and the six tall stacks of the boilers that fed the steam pumps, the top of each stack outlined in reddish glow. Far over, where the valley broke away, was the Winkin Jack property, but Kendall could not make it out in the glow of the starlit night. No lights at the Jack. Two years, Tarow had told him. since the underground river had broken into the Jack and sealed six dead men in the depth of its workings.

The still clear night, the sweep of the valley, the pattern of lights below him brought an odd, uplifting excitement to Kendall. It brought home the fact that upon Blue Grouse hung the fate of the little city, the fortunes of most of its people. They had made up the final chunk of the guarantee it took to get Blue Grouse going, beyond the backing of Tarow and Hagen and the Luscon Syndicate. To them. Blue Grouse was more than a hole in the rock. If it failed, water would overcome the costly steam pumps and drown out the Case Ace, with the Queen to follow, though its miners were a group apart in Juniper. And now Blue Grouse meant Mike Kendall. These people were depending on him. He swore softly. He hoped he wouldn't let them down. God knows I'll try, he thought.

Facing the window, he raised his glass in a toast to the town. And beside him the pane smashed in a shattering implosion. A flying sliver slashed his cheek as he dropped. On the far side of the room the grandfather clock blew apart in a chaos of broken metal and shattered mechanism. As if crying its wounds, the clock began striking with wild, erratic chimes.

Above Kendall another pane smashed. On the long table a crystal pitcher flew into daggered shards. Someone cried out.

"Get down!" Kendall yelled. Crouching, he ran to the doorway, snapped the switch that put out one of the great teardrop chandeliers. But the second one stayed on, and he could not see the switch. He picked up a chair and sprang onto the table, careless of silver and china and napery. He crashed the chair against the chandelier. It went out in a shower of tinkling fragments. As the room plunged into darkness, something tugged at his sleeve and slammed into the far wall.

He jumped down from the table. In the flat unreal silence, he found himself wondering what Ruth Hagen would think of the shambles he had made of the handsome table. He moved across the room toward the gray square of the window. The insane clock whirred, clicked, and began striking again.

He fumbled along the window edge. He pulled the cord, and the heavy drapes slid across the window. He did the same at the other window, and the room went from gray darkness to the blackness of a mine pit. "All right," he said.

Hagen scratched a match. In the sudden yellow flare Kendall saw the flat astonishment of the faces.

"All right, gentlemen," Hagen said calmly. "Let us join the ladies."

"Before someone else drygulches us," van Zandt said.

"But who was it?" Dooley Swain demanded. "Why? What did—"

"There's no story yet, Mr. Swain," Kendall said, turning the newspaperman toward the light of the inner hall. As Swain walked toward the parlor, Kendall could hear the man fizzing like a lemon phosphate in his impatience.

The women were excited and a little frightened. Martha Hagen ran to her husband, clung to him, her face ashen. "Oh, Aaron, you're not hurt? What on earth happened?"

Hagen put his arm around his wife. "My dear, calm yourself. Some unknown rifleman shot three or four times into the room while we were sitting there. No damage, I think, except to your Spode and your crystal. And he wounded the grandfather clock."

"I'm shot in the arm, Hagen," Lock Graney said plaintively.

Hagen looked at the man, Tarow's accountant. The seep of blood on the man's sleeve was slight. Hagen moved toward the telephone on the wall.

"Dr. Von Bulow will fix you up, Graney," he said. He took the receiver off the hook and spun the crank. "Hi, Millie. Get me Pete Trump, will you? In a hurry. No, nothing serious. No, dammit, I said—listen in, then, if you want to know. Hello, Pete. Say, we just had some wild shooting out at the house...."

As her father made his report, Ruth Hagen came to Kendall, concern on her face. "Mr. Kendall, were you hit? There's blood on your cheek."

Surprised, Kendall put up his hand. He felt the sticky wetness on his cheek, the grittiness of drying blood on his collar. Must be a gory mess, he thought. But this girl doesn't turn a hair.

"Flying glass, I think," he told her. "On my phiz it won't matter. But I must look like a slaughterhouse. Could I clean up?"

"Come with me," she said. "We'll get Dr. Von Bulow to look at it as soon as he finishes with Mr. Graney."

He followed her up the graceful curving sweep of the stair. The room they entered was flowery and feminine, Ruth Hagen's bedroom, he was sure. He took the chair she indicated, feeling a little out of place in this boudoir redolent of lavender and mignonette, a room shining and orderly, like the girl herself.

She made him lean back while she worked gently on the wound with water and soft cloths and a pungent antiseptic. As she leaned over Kendall he could not avoid, nor did he try, seeing the swelling loveliness her low-cut dinner gown revealed. No sham nor trickery to this girl, he thought, she—

Liquid fire bit at his cheek, and he winced.

"I'm sorry," she said, secret laughter in her voice. "It must have been the antiseptic. Here, hold this."

She lifted his hand against a wet pad across his cheek. The burning died to a dull glow. "I'll fetch Dr. Von Bulow now," she said, and hurried out in a rustle of taffeta.

He grimaced, stretching his cheek, feeling the sting of the antiseptic. She handed it to me, he thought. But it was worth it. Women have their own rules. They wear dresses like that, then resent it when we admire their charms. Keeping us in our place, I guess. Well, the game goes on.

She came back with the doctor. As he looked at Kendall's cheek, Kendall asked, "How's Graney?" Not that he cared much, for he had disliked Tarow's office manager from the time he had set eyes on him.

"Not enough to make a baby cry yet," the bearded doctor said, reaching for his bag. "This now—a pooty clean job. Nize clean cut, like mit vun of my scalpels." He threaded a curved needle.

"Brace yourself, Mr. Kendall. Now den—ve take vun stitch, so—den anudder, so—yah, it hurts all right—now vun more. And de chob is done. A few days, ve take de needlevork oudt, your face is good as new. Gives a nize scar, eh, Ruthie? Choost like the vuns de lads make for demselves at the University in Chermany. But vit sabers, yet. Not dat you need more scars, young man." He patted Kendall on the shoulder and began putting his instruments away. "Now, tell Doc Von Bulow—v'y vas dey shooting at you?"

Kendall felt reaction now, dizziness and a slight nausea. The doctor's question drove it out of mind.

"At me? Nobody shot at me, Doc. Where did you get that?"

"Not you, so? Ve look at de bullet holes. Ruthie's papa, or Jason Tarow, or you, young man."

"No reason to shoot at me," Kendall said, and meant it.

"Nor Daddy," Ruth insisted.

"Leaving Jason," the doctor said, cheerfully. "But vot an atrocious marksman de man vas. He hits glassvare, and Lock Graney, and de grandfadder clock. Even dat he choost vounds. Ruthie, I think your papa has to take dat clock out and kill it. Choost now it strikes thirty-nine o'clock!"

The doctor winked at them, grabbed his bag, and went out.

Kendall stood up, surprised to find that he was a little shaky. "Miss Ruth, I've caused a mess in your pretty room. Can I help to clean it up?"

"The maid will take care of it," she told him. She moved closer, touching his arm. "The truth, Mr. Kendall," she said. "Was it Jason? Or Daddy?"

"I've been in Juniper a week," he reminded her. "I can't answer your question. I suppose that in every town there are undercurrents and enmities and feuds, even deadly ones, that seldom come into the open. You would know better than I."

"I suppose that's true," she said, frowning. "Daddy has enemies, I know. Some in Juniper resent his good fortune, knowing he came up out of the Butte mines to make a successful gamble on the Case Ace. They refuse to believe that most of the several millions he made has gone back into development, into equipment, and now into your Blue Grouse tunnel. The tunnel means as much to us as to the rest of Juniper. So I can't think of a soul who would try to kill Daddy—or Jason. To hate them enough for murder." She shuddered.

"It beats me, Miss Ruth," he said. "Shall we go down now?"

They found Lock Graney being questioned by a fat man with a marshal's badge pinned awry on his stained vest.

"For the tenth time, McGown, I don't know a thing about it," Graney said irritably. "He wasn't shooting at me."

"Well, you was the one that got shot," the marshal said.

A slim, compact man with a taut, wise face moved in. "Let him be, Noble," he said. "We'll learn more in the morning, after we've checked the town and the place the shooting came from."

"All right, Pete. But there's folks here ain't tellin' all they know about this," the marshal said darkly. "Here's another all bunged up, but I betcha we won't even get the time of day outen him."

The slim man reached out a hand to Kendall. "I'm Pete Trump, sheriff of Quartz County. You're Kendall? I hear you got the lights out when the shooting started. Nice work. I don't suppose you have either facts or theories?"

Kendall shook his head. "I'm afraid you're right. I was looking out the window and it burst in my face. Then I ducked."

"Any guess as to the target?"

"It seemed mighty damned general to me," Kendall said.

When the lawmen had left, Tarow came up to Kendall and Ruth Hagen. "I'm sorry to let you down, Kendall, but I have business to talk with Aaron Hagen. Can you get back to the hotel all right?"

"Sure, don't let that bother you. In fact, I think I'll head out now. I'm dog tired."

Ruth Hagen went to the door with him. "Good night, Mr. Kendall," she said, giving him her hand.

"Make it Mike," he said. "May I see you again, Miss Ruth?"

"I'd like that," she said.

As he was about to turn away, a thought occurred to him.

"Miss Ruth, does van Zandt feel strongly enough to try to stop the tunnel by hiring gunmen?" he asked.

"He is tough and cold," she said, "and he makes no bones about his opposition to Blue Grouse. Yes, he might go to any lengths."

"It would pay a man to mind his p's and q's in Juniper, then."

"Have faith, Mr. Kendall, but keep your powder dry," she said.

She was still silhouetted in the yellow light of the doorway as he went out the gate and turned toward the town.

CHAPTER THREE

In the blackness of the night the road was a lighter blackness. The dust of it was a soft resilience under Kendall's shoes. The dark loom against the star-glow to his left was the shoulder of a hill. It would, he thought, overlook the Hagen dining room. From it somewhere, had come the shots.

He felt the breath of a cool breeze, he felt naked and exposed. Involuntarily he quickened his pace, though he knew that he would be a poor target in his dark clothing. Nor would a sniper with any slight lick of sense linger around the vicinity. But he moved faster all the same.

The road straightened down the slope toward the jeweled lights below. Ahead of Kendall a shadow moved. He checked his step, his heart jumping.

"That you, Kendall?" came the sheriff's pleasant voice.

Kendall let out his pent breath in a long sigh.

"It's me all right," he said. "But Lord, Pete Trump, you might as well kill a man as scare him to death."

"Well, you got no business prowling in the dark by your lonesome. Tarow brought you. Why ain't he taking you back to the hotel in his rig?"

"I told him I'd make it; he had business with Hagen. Besides, I needed the walk. Seven-course dinner, four kinds of wine. Pretty rich for my blood after construction camp fare."

"Better'n flying lead, too. Wisht you'd be careful, Kendall. Juniper needs you as well as Jase Tarow."

"Engineers are a dime a dozen," Kendall told him.

"Your kind? I doubt that. Besides, there would be all the lost time while we dug up another man."

"Plant one and dig up another, eh? Pleasant thought for a night after being shot at. Any inkling as to our gunman?"

"Just that he used a .44-40. I'll take another look in the morning. Wisht I knew who he was trying for—it would make it some easier," Trump said, with a certain grumpiness.

"Maybe he just hates people," Kendall said.

"Got a couple birds around here would even qualify on that score. Claude Lamb, f'rinstance. He could've borrowed Eddie's rifle, it's the right caliber. He'd use it, too. Had him in the juzgado a couple times for promiscuous shooting."

"Who might this Claude Lamb be?"

"One of our local crackbrains. Miner, prospector, hunter, in the off season a hellfire and damnation preacher of no particular persuasion. Anybody else would be down to Warm Springs. But we tolerate Claude because he takes care of his nephew, Eddie, after a fashion. You see, Eddie's pa, Claude's brother, was lost when the Winkin Jack flooded. Eddie himself was the only person come out alive the night the water busted in."

"How did he manage that?"

"Far as anybody can tell, by a plumb miracle. It'll stay at that, I guess. There's no way to get a story out of the boy."

"Why not?"

"Struck dumb, Kendall. The doc explains it with a long lingo, but to say it plain, the kid can't say a word since the night two years ago when he come crawling, all blood, out of the Winkin Jack shaft. Good kid, though. Never bothers nobody."

They were in front of the hotel now. The sheriff reached out a hand as calloused and rough as old horn. "Glad to have made your acquaintance, Kendall. Take *good* care of yourself."

From the steps Kendall watched Trump head down the street toward the county jail. Lean and salty, he thought. A man any wrongdoer would hate to have on his trail.

The next morning he was breakfasting early in the hotel dining room when Pete Trump came up to the table and pulled out a chair.

"Have something, Sheriff?" Kendall asked.

Trump shook his head. He concentrated on rolling a brown paper cigarette.

"Ate a couple hours ago. I wanted to get up the hill as soon as the sun come up."

"Any luck?"

Trump fished with thumb and forefinger into a vest pocket. He tossed a cylinder of dull brass onto the table. Kendall picked it up.

".44-40, all right. On that rock shoulder east of the house," Trump told him. "Now I have to find the rifle."

Kendall handed back the shell. "You think this Eddie Lamb had a hand in it?"

The sheriff shook his head. He tossed the brass cylinder in the air and caught it.

"Uh-uh. First off, Eddie wouldn't hurt a fly. And in the next place if Eddie thrown four slugs through Hagen's window at you, you wouldn't be here, mister. You'd be dead."

That day Kendall finished his resurvey. He had insisted, over Tarow's objections, on running out levels and corners and locations, step by slow step. When he paid off his rodmen and chainman that night, he was satisfied. The original work had been done by a man fairly competent in land survey, but rather slipshod in the niceties of a mining survey. Two errors in contour, though small, might have been expensive. And one faulty tie corrected by Kendall could have cost an added fifty thousand dollars in excavation.

He had been using his hotel room as an office. Now he went to the window. Looking down the street, he saw a light in the office of Blue Grouse Development. He rolled up his maps and papers and went downstairs.

Fran Diamond looked up from her work as he entered the office. She was neat in dark skirt and crisp white shirtwaist. I suppose, Kendall thought, she wasn't invited to the Hagen's last night because she is a working girl. He had an idea of the rigid caste system in these mining towns. Only when she was Mrs. Jason Tarow would this girl be accepted.

"Hi, Miss Diamond," he said. "Is the Little Giant in?"

She inclined her head toward the inner office. "And I wish you wouldn't call him that, Mr. Kendall."

"It was good enough for Stephen Douglas, and he was a great man," Kendall said.

She tossed her head and turned back to her typewriter, making the office echo with its staccato clatter. He stood watching a moment, admiring her virtuosity. Few, if any, typists could match that speed. The machine, he saw, had visible writing, so it was one of the newest models. He hoped Tarow would be as generous with machinery for the tunnel work.

He went into Tarow's office. The promoter pushed papers away, and motioned toward a chair. His eyes were weary. Kendall made his report, unrolling maps to illustrate his points.

"Good work," Tarow said when they were through. "You were right again, Mike. Now we can begin with a sure foundation. How soon, Mike, do you think?"

"How about the camp?"

"Ready in another three days, Kryder tells me. Two bunkhouses, cookshack, stables, storage shed, your quarters combined with an office, and the other smaller buildings."

"More than I expected of Kryder," Kendall said.

"Now, Mike, he's a good man. Maybe gruff and unpolished, but a good man. Why, he's been with me ..."

"I know," Kendall interrupted, "since you bought that Apex claim, found a stringer, and sold it in your first big coup. I swear, Jason, that big gorilla is the weirdest good luck charm I ever saw. You've got more fetishes than a Bantu tribesman."

He jerked a thumb toward the outer office. "Is she another one?"

Tarow's face lighted. "Why, she's my finest charm of all. I couldn't get along without Fran. And Mike, when this job is brought to success, I'm going to do something about that."

"More power to you." Kendall said. "Now, how about starting to move machinery tomorrow?"

The straining ox teams had brought first the steam engine, then the compressor down the long steep grades into Blue Grouse Canyon without incident. It took tackle and snubbing ropes and rough locks on all the wagon wheels, but there had been no mishap. The millwrights were setting the machinery up on the bench across the creek from the tunnel adit, well above high water.

But the boiler was another story. It was a brute of a thing, ungainly in every dimension, top-heavy, its round bulk the very devil to tie down. Kendall put together the running gears of two great ore wagons and joined them with a cradle of solid oak. Onto this he skidded the boiler, blocked it, chained it, and boomed down the chains. He had the whole thing brought taut with driven maple wedges. He rallied a double crew of men, hooked on twelve spans of oxen, and started over the hills toward Blue Grouse.

The road turned away from the Carden River just out of town and began to climb. On the Juniper side, it was steep enough, rough with rocks, with switchbacks climbing through the timber to the crest of the ridge. But the far side was hellish. It dropped down the mountainside without proper room or grade, clinging to bare cliffs and edging around solid outcrops. It couldn't be helped—bad as it was, it was the only feasible supply route from Juniper to the Blue Grouse. Something over twelve miles of road. Looking down from the crest, Kendall felt again the amazement that when the tunnel was finished, it would join the same two points in two and a half miles.

He was walking with the men. He was as sweaty, as dirty, as parched as they were. He wanted to be Johnny-on-the-spot if any trouble occurred. And more, he had to show the men he was equal to any job he might ask of them. It was a trick of leadership he had learned from Morley. But, Mike Kendall thought wryly, for Morley it was easy, with his giant frame and inexhaustible stamina. Mike, wiry and tough as he was, had to work at appearing fresh and eager when his whole body was aching with fatigue.

The huge rig was pulling up to the crest of the ridge. Mike walked on ahead, down the deceptively easy first slant. He found the little spring and drank sparingly of its icy water. He rinsed the sweat and dust from his face and sat down with his back against a tree, hat in hand to ward off the deerflies. Relaxing, he was dimly conscious of the sound of teams and wagons and noisy men, knowing that the instant a discordant note touched his ear he would be instantly alert. He let his thoughts drift.

He thought of Ruth Hagen. He had visited at her house in the past week. He and Aaron Hagen had talked shop for a bit, then he and Ruth had played Russian bank. She had beaten him badly. Later they had gone for a walk in the fine spring night. Ruth had led the way to a vista point on the hill above the house. Bright moonlight was flooding the valley below. On the far slopes the tailings dumps made white scars in the black of the jack pines.

Ruth spread her skirts and sank onto the rustic bench.

"Mike, isn't it a marvelous night?" she sighed. "To think that there are people who would give up all this for the noise and the smoke of cities."

"Each to his own taste, Ruth. I don't doubt many people here in Juniper would move to a city at the drop of a hat."

"I'm afraid you're right," she said, turning toward him, her face a shadowed oval in the soft light. "Which spoils my wise pretensions. I know one woman who would sell her soul for city life—Thelma van Zandt."

"Perhaps she thinks her beauty is wasted here," Kendall said. "And she is beautiful. She would be a sensation in the salons of New York or San Francisco."

"Strange, isn't it? For Thelma is cruel and hard and utterly selfish. Some of it I blame on Phil van Zandt. Living with that money-mad boor would try the character of any woman."

"I don't like the man. But if she is typical of Montana—"

"Do you find the rest of us ugly, then, good sir?"

"Heavens no, Ruth," he said hastily. "On the contrary, the average is extraordinarily high. Why, just at random—Katie, who waits table at the Elkhorn; that redhaired niece of the banker's; your teacher friend, Miss Demarett; Pete Trump's wife, Helen; and of course your lovely self. Oh, and another, Fran Diamond."

"Why, Mike, how very democratic of you," Ruth said, a cold edge in her voice.

"You challenge my judgment?" he asked.

"Not at all. Every one of them is—well, very beautiful. But I'm not sure I'm flattered at being included in such a cosmopolitan list."

"Good Lord, Ruth, does it offend you to be named in the same breath as a secretary, a waitress, a teacher?" he demanded, angry as much at his mistake in judging her character as at her words. "I won't withdraw it—you are all beautiful women. I haven't been long enough in Juniper to judge any of you by your station in life—or by your morals." He stood up, turning away.

She came quickly to her feet. She put her hands on his arms, facing him, her eyes gleaming in the pale light.

"Mike, I'm not like that, honestly. Please forgive me. I do agree with you. It is just that—Mike, I think you will find as little snobbishness in me as in any woman, but I have intensely personal feelings toward two of those on your list. Thelma van Zandt I pity and avoid and loathe. The other—she came up out of abject poverty by her own raw courage and brains and mother wit. For what she is and what she has I envy her and I fear her. She has abilities and character I can never match. You'll never know—oh, Mike, let's go back."

He took her arm. "And her name?" he asked.

"Fran Diamond."

CHAPTER FOUR

By the noise, the heavy rig was nearing the top of the ridge. Kendall got stiffly to his feet and started back, walking in the shade beside the road. Around the bend in a clatter of hoofs came two horses, magnificent star-blazed blacks, almost identical.

Phil van Zandt rode one of them, his wife Thelma the other. Kendall looked at her admiringly. In velvet riding habit, she sat side saddle on the big horse, straight, magnificent. She nodded imperiously to Kendall.

Van Zandt pulled his horse to a curvetting stop. "So, Kendall, you never give up," he said. "You're going through with it."

"What did you think?" Kendall asked in surprise.

"Until now, most likely one of Tarow's blue-sky promotions. But only damned fools work as hard as you do. I believe you are in earnest."

"You thought we were running a sandy? That's sheer stupidity, van Zandt."

The man's bronzed face darkened with anger.

"The stupidity is yours in disregarding my warning. Kendall, you'll learn sooner or later that Phil van Zandt never bluffs. Before you have to learn the hard way, I'll renew my offer to pay your ticket out of town."

Kendall shook his head. He looked up at the man towering over him.

"You know better, van Zandt. But you puzzle me. Tell me honestly, why do you object so strenuously to draining the Castle

Lode? It will help all of Juniper if we get the Case Ace back into profitable figures, and reopen the Winkin Jack."

The big man surveyed him with cold contempt. "Kendall, get this through your head—I'm not going to stand still for anyone tampering with the underground geology of Castle Mountain. I don't care that the Jack is closed forever, nor that Hagen has to use expensive steam pumps, to keep the Case Ace from flooding. All I care about is that the Queen o' Hearts took a million and a half out of the Castle Lode last year. Nobody nor nothing is going to jeopardize that kind of production. Do you understand?"

Again the man's arrogance whipped the anger in Kendall.

"I do not," he said. "Why should it be any skin off your nose if we drain the Lode? In fact, it relieves you of any future threat of underground water, for free. And any good rock hound will tell you there isn't a chance of damage to your holdings from our tunnel."

"I don't argue with hired hands," van Zandt said. "Just be assured that I will back my position to the hilt. And if you still don't understand, Kendall, *there will be signs to convince you. Watch for them!*"

He dragged his horse back on its haunches, swinging it. The steel-shod hoofs flung dangerously close to Kendall's face.

"Come, Thelma," van Zandt called over his shoulder. He spurred the black toward the ridge top in a swirl of dust.

Thelma van Zandt did not hurry. She sat her horse quietly, looking at Kendall with the slightest of smiles on her perfect features.

Kendall jerked a thumb toward the horseman. "A man of sudden furies, Mrs. van Zandt," he said.

She leaned forward and stroked the sleek neck of her horse. Negligently she said, "Phil is a damned dangerous brute. Mr. Mike Kendall. He has a wicked streak of cruelty in him. I tell you that from positive knowledge. So please don't discount his warning as empty words. Since Phil has this terrible hate for your tunnel plan, I would advise you to get out of Juniper—now. The Blue Grouse is foredoomed to failure."

He shook his head. "I refuse to believe that, Mrs. van Zandt. And since I was hired to make it succeed, I intend to see to it."

She shrugged. "I pity you, Mike Kendall. You are stubbornly obtuse. I'll be more blunt—before Phil van Zandt permits the tunnel to be completed, he will eliminate you and Jason Tarow."

"You are implying violence? Murder?"

"Something less crude than that, Mr. Kendall," she said, the soft smile still on her lips. "But at the end of it, both you and that cunning little man will be dead."

Kendall felt a prickling at the back of his neck. This woman wasn't joking. She meant what she said. What manner of woman was she, that she could live on with a monster like van Zandt?

She must have read his thought. For the briefest of instants her mask slipped. Smoldering hate twisted her face.

"Phil van Zandt is a devil worthy of Satan himself," she began. Then she brought her emotions under control. "But, Mr. Kendall, he is worth several million dollars. And I am his wife."

She straightened in the sidesaddle. She touched the black with her riding crop, turned him with a gentle rein. She looked back over her shoulder.

"Goodbye, Mr. Kendall. You are the first man in five long years to shake my self-control. Don't let such a gift be wasted by suicidal stubbornness. Leave Juniper."

She brought the riding crop up in salute. Shaking the black into a trot, she rode away up the trail.

Kendall stood looking after her through the dust that hung in the still, hot air. He felt somewhat shaken. The malevolence of van Zandt was an evil, tangible thing.

And the eerie nonchalance of Mrs. van Zandt was not within his ordinary experience. This, he thought, is a part of the undercurrent I sensed in Juniper. And I don't like the shape it is taking.

As he walked back up the road to meet the ox teams there seemed to be a chill in the air.

Tarow's man, Drag Kryder, met him. A great hulk of muscle, the man was not old, but his great head was bald as a turkey egg. He came stumping through the dust on pillars of legs, his torn shirt open to the waist, showing the tangled mat of hair on his chest.

"How's it going, Kryder?" Kendall asked.

"So far, so good," Kryder said, his voice oddly high of pitch.

"I checked the road," Kendall said. "The roughlocks will get us by to the little spring. Then we'll split the teams, putting two spans ahead and eight spans behind. Farther down we'll have to use the anchor trees. I've marked them. Get your tackle set up, with good stout men on the lines. I want the rig kept moving smartly, to get it down to water level by nightfall."

"She'll get there," Kryder promised, grinning.

"And pick out four men, you know the ones, for that wheeled wedge. I want them alert and ready."

Kryder snorted. "That jigger's a waste of time. I could use the men better on the fall lines."

"Never mind that. I saw it save a rig in Oregon once. Get the men on it."

Kryder was scowling and grumbling as he left.

The spring afternoon slid away. They fought the monstrous bulk of the boiler down grade and switch-back with the brute muscle of men and oxen, now alone, now multiplied by the ingenious leverage of tackle and rigging. Weary, killing work, all of it. But slowly the rig creaked down toward Blue Grouse. At the head of the last steep pitch, with the sun slanting low through a gap in the hills, Kendall called a halt.

"Let's take five," he called.

Men flopped down against wagon wheels, or onto the blanket of pine needles, as if to gather from the earth a new charge of energy.

Kendall motioned Kryder over. The big man stood, his jaws working on a Gargantuan cud of tobacco. He spat downwind. He stood waiting, his thumbs hooked in his belt.

Kendall said, "Once more, Kryder. I want no slip-ups. This is the worst pitch of all, then we're home. It's straight, too damn' straight. It's the creek away down and the cliff away up, nothing but a shelf of rock for the road. We'll count on the oxen, and a straight snub to that anchor tree. It's right in line with the pitch."

"You got fifteen hundred feet of two-inch hawser, ain't you?" Kryder asked. "That oughtta hold a clipper ship, let alone a double wagon."

"It will. But it has a certain amount of give to it. And we'll have to block the rig while we take a new purchase, every time we two-block the tackle. So watch it. I'm counting on you up here, I'll be down below. If you even suspect trouble starting, yell to make the hills echo. Don't wait."

"Cut your worrying, Kendall," Kryder said. "I know what I'm doing. I'll let 'er down easy."

"You damn' well better," Kendall growled. "The nearest boiler like this one is in Butte. Any damage will set our whole schedule back for weeks, maybe months. Look sharp, now."

He waited until the men had started uncoiling the end of the great Manila hawser, so new it shone gold in the slanting light. When the big blocks had been rigged, he was satisfied. He went on down to the wagons and lined up the bullwhackers, both old hands at this sort of thing. He found the four men with the rolling wedge were ready, having practiced the exact moves they would need to thrust the wedge under to block the rig if anything went wrong.

One last look at the layout, and Kendall waved his hat in a circle over his head. The bullwhackers popped leather out over the oxen. Tackle creaked as it took up the slack. With slow grating and grinding, the huge outfit began inching down. Kendall moved ahead.

Forty feet the rig made before the tackle two-blocked. The wedges went under the wheels, the men ran out a new purchase on the rope. Then the descent began again, agonizingly slow, the awkward load teetering perilously on the narrow road. Kendall watched every detail, holding his breath at times. For a single miscue could drop the wagons, oxen and men headlong into the depths of the canyon.

Four times they lowered and stopped. On the fifth leg, the rig nosed into the steepest pitch of the hill. Kendall relaxed a little. He was walking at the head end when a noise made him wheel around, his eyes questing. It came again, a soft snapping sound. The rig lurched. The oxen grunted. Far up the hill someone yelled.

Kendall saw the iron-hard bar of the hawser dip, slacken, jerk taut. He felt the cold breath of disaster and he did not wait. "Wedge! Dammit, wedge!" he yelled.

As if they had practiced for days, the four men swung the cart with its V-wedge of timber. They shoved it under the rear wheels of the lead wagon. Exactly as planned, the light wheels crumpled under the oncoming weight. The slanting ground spikes dug solidly into the road surface. The great wheels, almost as high as a man, struck the timber balk and rose up on it. Then they sagged back. The rig stopped dead.

In that very second the hawser parted with the crack of a gunshot. The frayed end slashed downhill toward the rig. Kendall dove flat into the dust, heedless of rock chips grinding into his face. Above him the hawser end cut the air like the hiss of a blacksnake whip. There was a thud. An ox bawled and was silent.

Kendall got up slowly. He brushed grime and gravel from his clothes. Men were swarming around the wagons. An ox was down in its yoke. The skinner was trying to get it up, turning the air blue with his blasphemy. Grim-faced, Kendall turned up the hill.

Irish Murfree, recently hired as carpenter and rigger fore-man, met him on the slope.

"Boss, the hawser snapped like butcher's twine. The end of it just missed you, skulled yon ox like a stone from a catapult. I niver thought it possible of brand-new Manila."

"Nor I," Kendall said, picking up the end of the rope. It was frayed like the end of a cow's tail. The two men fanned out the lay of the cable.

"Holy Mother, Mr. Kendall!" the Irishman exclaimed, "She didn't break by herself atall, atall. Some spalpeen chopped her half through. Which might have killed all of us, God save us."

Black anger filled Kendall. He strode on up the hill to the place where the tackle crew stood milling.

"None of you hurt? Good. That's more important than wag-ons or boilers. Now, did anyone see a sign of tampering with this rope?"

The men looked at each other uncertainly. Finally one stepped forward. "It ain't my practice to tell tales out of school," he said diffidently. "But this coulda killed a man or two. So I got to say it—just before she went, I seen Drag Kryder fooling around on the line of the cable. In that clump of bresh there."

Kendall thrust alder limbs aside to where a fallen log crossed the path of the hawser. There was a fresh scar in its rotten bark. In the loam beside it lay a new hatchet. Kendall picked it up, ran the ball of his thumb along its edge. Razor sharp. He handed it to Murfree.

"A souvenir for you, Irish," he said flatly. He gave a hitch to the belt of his pants. "Has anyone seen Drag Kryder?"

"Right here, Kendall," came Kryder's high-pitched voice from the road above them. "You want me for something?"

Kendall looked up at the big man. Kryder grinned down, standing solidly on those great pillars of legs. He flexed his arms, moved his shoulders. He stood waiting.

Kendall flicked a thumb toward the rope's end.

"Is this your work, Kryder?"

"Well, now, a man would be a fool to admit that. But I tell you, sonny boy, I ain't denying it, neither."

"You're certainly loyal to Jason Tarow," Kendall said, walking up the hill toward the man.

"That's what Jase thought," the giant said with a chuckle. Feller's s'posed to be grateful all his life for one small favor, I guess. Well, I ain't that kind. I can make a hell of a lot better money, and easier, than by taking orders from that little tarrier. I'm a big man, Kendall. I'm gonna do big things."

"On whose orders?"

"I ain't saying. But I can give you one piece of advice, Scarface, free, gratis and for nothing. Quit and get out of Juniper while your skin is still in one piece. You'll never finish the Blue Grouse."

"They hang men for murder in Montana, Kryder," Kendall said, his voice cold. "You nearly set yourself up for it a few minutes ago. Better think it over before you make another bad move." He was on the road now, a few feet from the big man.

"You can't scare me, Scarface," Kryder jeered. "I got backing that'll clear me of any trouble from the law from now on. I'm in clover, sonny." He laughed again.

Kendall eyed the man without enthusiasm. David and Goliath, he thought, but I haven't got a slingshot. Still I've got to make my move, or lose all standing with this crew. And be licked at Blue Grouse before I start.

Without warning, he struck with flashing speed. He rammed a knee into Kryder's paunch. As the man lurched Kendall hit him with a left to the throat and a right to the cheek. He hammered home the left again and tried to duck back.

Bellowing, Kryder made his move, startlingly fast for a man so outsized. He caught Kendall in his great hands, shook him, flung him away. Kendall came up out of the brush clump scratched, bleeding, but full of fight. He started after Kryder.

But his men were ahead of him. With shovels, peavey handles, cudgels and rocks, they were closing in on Drag Kryder, stalking him like wolves after a bull elk. He was retreating, step by slow step. Someone threw a rock. It bounced harmlessly off the man's shoulder.

Still, it must have frightened Kryder. His hand slipped into his shirt front, came out with a gleam of metal. The bulldog revolver looked like a toy in that Gargantuan hand.

"Stay back, you fools," he said, swinging the gun. But the arc of men moved closer.

"Hold it, boys," Kendall said. "I wouldn't want any one of you to suffer hurt at the hands of this ape. He's done his worst. Let him go."

"That's mighty smart of you, Kendall," Kryder said, backing off. "Better get smarter still and check out of this job."

"You haven't thought this thing through, Kryder," Kendall said. "You don't want me to do that. You couldn't get paid for these filthy little tricks of yours then, with nobody to play them on. Why, Kryder, I'm the same as money in the bank for you, as long as we're working at Blue Grouse. But while you're thinking up your next deviltry, keep this in mind—don't get caught on our side of the mountain, *ever*. If you should, you can be very sure that nobody in this world will ever see you again. And that, Kryder, is not idle talk."

There was a chorus from the men. Fear for his life finally hit Kryder, and hit him hard. His face contorted with it, and he ran clumsily up the road and ducked into the trees. Murfree made a motion to go after him but Kendall put a hand on his arm. In a minute Kryder came riding out of the woods into the open, astride a horse well suited to pulling a dray. But Kryder was spurring hard. They went pounding out of sight up the ridge.

Kendall spat into the dust. "That's good riddance, boys. Now, Irish, you boasted you were an old deepwater man. Ten dollars says you can't splice that hawser navy fashion in less than an hour."

Murfree grinned at Kendall. He spat on his hands. "Done and done, Mr. Kendall, sir. Get your money ready, clear the way, and have the boys bring me the ends of yon skipping rope!"

CHAPTER FIVE

In his work with Jason Tarow, Kendall came to realize how the promoter could sell a project like Blue Grouse to his influential backers. Tarow had a friendliness, a persuasiveness, that could charm a bird from a tree. But like many men who are smaller than average in stature, he had a sort of gadfly persistence with which he harassed Kendall to attain his object.

"But Mike," he insisted, "it would only mean eight days. Just think, all our stockholders, all of Juniper celebrating the Glorious Fourth, the celebration capped by the great official blast opening the construction of Blue Grouse. Everybody welcome, free beer for the men, free soda for the ladies and children, plenty of food for all. Why, it'll be sensational."

"Except for one thing," Kendall said. "It isn't coming off."

"Dear me, Mike," Jason Tarow sighed. "You are stubborn."

Curbing his impatience, Kendall leaned across the desk. "Let me try once more, Jason. Point by point—the millwrights are through, the boiler and engine and compressor set are piped and tested. The hundred-and-twenty-five-pound air line is laid to the adit. The tram rails are laid, the drill jumbo is about finished. In the eight days before the Fourth we can push our drift well into the side of this mountain. You say yourself that every day counts."

"It does, of course. But I might sacrifice a few days' progress…"

"Point two, then—get a crowd into this narrow canyon, set off a blast, and somebody will get killed."

"Now, Mike. It would just be a token shot, a noise-maker."

"I'll grant you all those things," Kendall said grimly. He pointed a rigid forefinger at Tarow. "Then I'll make my last and most important point. I won't have an uncontrolled bunch of outsiders milling around my job. A handful of emery in an engine bearing, a match lighted and dropped in a corner, an essential part stolen from the compressor—or even a slow fuse into the powderhouse. I think I can count on my men. But from recent happenings, we can't count on everyone in Juniper."

"Drag Kryder was a bitter disappointment to me, I'll admit," Tarow said, shaking his head. "But he's only one man. So Mike, I think we'll go on with the celebration as I planned it."

Kendall stood up, putting his palms flat on the desk top. He leaned forward.

Jason, things have been moving toward this for the last ten days. You hired me at a high salary to run this job, promising full authority. Yet time and again you have countermanded my orders or argued my judgment. You're forcing me to an ultimatum, so here it is—I'm not going to work without the full authority you gave me."

Tarow met his glance squarely, a cold gleam in the usually kindly eyes.

"That full authority, Mike, was given to Morley Kendall. Since you are not that person, my promise is not binding."

"So Fran talked."

"Did she know also? It doesn't matter. When you didn't show the legendary personality of Big Morley Kendall, I made a few simple inquiries. They proved you a complete impostor."

"For impersonating myself?" Kendall demanded. "Jason, I never pretended to be Morley Kendall. I'm a competent engineer. I accepted a definite offer from you to run Blue Grouse. My work, I think, has proved that I can deliver the goods."

"But you are not Morley Kendall," Tarow said triumphantly.

"Which means?"

"That mine is the final decision. When I get back to Juniper I'll get out the handbills announcing the celebration on the Fourth."

Kendall shook his head. "By the Fourth of July, my crews will be two hundred feet into the rock of Castle Mountain."

"This is my project, Mike Kendall," Tarow said, his voice icy. "I've spent two years turning a dream into reality. I'm not going to have that dream turned into a nightmare by any cheap jackleg engineer."

"That does it then, Jason," Kendall said calmly. "Since the evening I brought the boiler safe into camp, not one day has passed without at least one of my orders being countermanded by either you or Lock Graney. Your interference is bad enough, but to have that tubercular counterjumper annoying me is intolerable."

He walked over to the wardrobe and took out a battered suitcase. He flung it open on the bed and began taking clothing out of the drawers of the bureau.

"Mike, what are you up to?" Tarow asked in alarm.

"You've made it plain enough. The men would say, 'He's being sent down the road talking to himself.' There's a night train out of Juniper. If I hurry I think I can make it."

"All this over a little argument? You would leave me and my investors in the lurch?"

Kendall dropped a handful of socks into the bag and came over to the desk.

"Jason, that proves you don't have the slightest conception of what it takes to run a job of this kind. There has to be one kingpin, one man running the show. You can call him superintendent, or pusher, or bull o' the woods. In any case, he's *The Man*. I thought that's what you hired me for. Yet you and Graney keep meddling in my domain. So you and Graney can punch this tunnel through Castle Mountain, or you can round up some other chump of an engineer. But I'm through, as of right now."

Jason Tarow's face was horrified. "Mike, you can't do this to me! I have the utmost confidence in you. You may not be a good diplomat, but you're a good engineer, you have shown that. Don't be hasty."

"I'm not bluffing, Jason. This watered-down version of authority won't do. If there are contradictory orders, the job will slow down, the costs will go up, and worst of all, sooner or later someone will get killed because of it. I'll stay with Blue Grouse only if I am restored to full authority—and keep it."

Jason Tarow sighed. He pulled a pad of paper toward him.

"I know when I'm licked, Mike." He scribbled swiftly, signed his name, and handed the sheet to Kendall. "Here you are, Mike. A guarantee of full authority to make all decisions on the job. And a rider that permits me to fire you instanter if you stumble."

Kendall folded the paper and placed it in his wallet. He tried not to show his satisfaction. "Thanks, Jason. My first request under this agreement is going to gravel you. I want Lock Graney out of this camp, and I want him out damn quick."

"I don't know about that," Tarow said, frowning. "Good accountants are hard to come by. Why do you want to get rid of him? By any chance do you think you can hoodwink some green hand?"

"You know better than that, Jason," Kendall said angrily. "I want him out because Graney is a gossip in pants, because he is sly and calculating and a perpetual troublemaker. Even in this short time he has gotten the men stirred up on two occasions. He's a master of breeding enmity. I'm through with him."

"But who will handle orders and payrolls, and inventories and progress reports? I want progress reports every day and a complete cost report every week. With Graney gone ..."

"That's your problem. One thing. I'm running a telephone line over the hump to Juniper. You'll be in touch with us at all times."

"Mike, I swear, you're going to bankrupt us. A telephone line. You want the drills gold-plated, too?"

"It'll pay off. Wait and see."

Jason Tarow shook his head in mock despair. "All right, Mike. You win. Ride over me roughshod. Spend my money like water. What do I care? I can start over with grease rag and oilcan."

Kendall grinned at him, saying nothing. Tarow sat staring at the window, the picture of a broken man. Then a gleam came into his eyes. He snapped his fingers and chuckled.

"You'll hornswoggle me, will you. Mike Kendall? Well, I'll get even. I'll send you an accountant, a good one, one I can trust."

"That's what we need. Who is it?"

Tarrow looked at him slyly. "Fran Diamond," he said.

Kendall groaned. "You're joking, Jason. A young girl in the middle of a rough, tough construction camp! We may be snowed in for weeks this winter. What if she got sick? What if some of these hairy apes got ideas? Oh, hell, you can't do it. She wouldn't come anyway."

"Oh, yes she will, if I tell her. She hasn't any family left in Juniper, she could save on board and room out here. As for the other, Fran knows her way around men. She'll likely be a good sobering influence on these hardy souls. Don't beef, Mike. You started this thing. I'll finish it."

"Damnation!" Kendall said, giving the suitcase a kick that sent it against the wall. He came back to the desk. "You think this is smart? Sending your fiancée over here for a year?"

"It will give me an excuse to visit the job oftener," Tarow said. He was pleased with himself, Kendall saw. Suddenly the humor of the situation hit him. He began to laugh. After a moment, Tarow was laughing too.

Kendall thrust out a hand. "You're a hard man, Jason. Damned if I don't like you more every day."

The little man shook hands. "You're chilled steel and rawhide yourself, Mike. Let's smoke the peace pipe. And the celebration?"

"You can have it, mister. At half-past four tomorrow, with not more than ten guests, all of whom you can vouch for personally. The blast will be ready, but a real one. You can light the fuses yourself."

"A pleasure I'll forego," Tarow said hastily.

"A single exception to the list, though I'm sure you'll agree. I don't want either of the van Zandts within cannonshot of Blue Grouse."

"Depend on it. I didn't tell you, but he tangled with Aaron Hagen a few days ago. Made a lot of wild threats about closing down the job. Aaron was hopping mad. He told me van Zandt didn't have to participate in the tunnel, even though it helped him, but damned if the man was going to get anywhere with his crazy idea of stopping construction. He said van Zandt talked like a wild man."

"The man's dangerous, and so is his wife. She reminds me of a loaded round of powder with the fuse smoldering," Kendall said.

"She scares me," Tarow admitted, "but what a beautiful trollop she is. Plenty of men in Juniper would like to be in Sprague Laurens' shoes."

"You among them, Jason? I'm afraid she'd eat either of us alive. Doesn't van Zandt object to this lover of hers?"

"Apparently not. Laurens isn't the first. I think all Phil wants is to show her off as one of his beautiful possessions. Sometimes I think they hate each other."

"I think you're right. But she'll fight to protect van Zandt's fortune. A fine thing to speculate about—what would Fran say if she heard you mooning over the spectacular Thelma?"

"She'd be jealous, I hope," Jason Tarow said wistfully.

The late afternoon was quiet, after the day-long chatter of the Ingersolls. From this height Kendall could hardly make out the scars the drifters had punched into the solid rock. He shepherded the small group of people along the trail to a vantage point across the canyon and above the blast site and directed them behind the log barrier he had had Murfree erect for added safety. One never quite knew with dynamite.

He took Ruth Hagen's arm and helped her around some fallen rock. They came out onto the level back of the barrier.

"Thank you, Mike," she said, smiling at him. She turned toward the edge of the cliff and swept her arm toward the immensity of the scene below. "Isn't this marvelous, Mike? So big, so clean, so beautiful. How anyone would want to live in a city …"

"I agree with you," he said, "but did you ever try it?"

She shook her head. "As a matter of fact, I never have. Why, Mike, I might even like it!"

"Not you," he told her. He found her a place to sit on a cut log. "You can see from here, Ruth. I'll be back in a little bit."

More guests were coming up the steep path, some taking it in stride, others panting at the effort it took in the high, thin air. Tarow had stretched the limit a little, but he had the big names of Juniper—Lipscomb, the banker, his stout wife and pretty daughter; Dooley Swain of the *Prospector,* squiring Ruth's friend, the schoolteacher; Pete Trump and his wife; Dr. Von Bulow, impish as ever; Long Sam Carlson and two other well-fed backers of Tarow's Luscon Syndicate; Aaron Hagen without his wife, who must have been ailing again; and finally, Jason Tarow himself, with Fran Diamond. They crowded in on the small flat area of the viewpoint.

Tarow gave Kendall a preoccupied nod and hurried past to join Long Sam Carlson. Kendall was used to the little man's moods by this time and took no offense. Besides, he was anxious to speak to Fran alone.

"Fran, I didn't …" he began.

"No, no, you had nothing to do with me being exiled out in the hills," she said with indignation.

"I only said I wouldn't have Lock Graney on the job."

"Which left me," she said, scowling at him. Then her lovely face broke into a smile. She put a small strong hand on his arm. "I'm teasing, Mike. What girl wouldn't be happy to be exiled with a hundred men, some of them single? Right out in the middle of fine fishing and hunting and beautiful mountain scenery."

"It won't be a picnic," he said. "But Fran, I'm pleased to have you. I'm sure you'll be comfortable in the quarters we fixed."

He found her a seat, near where Jason was now talking in his absorbed fashion to Ruth Hagen. She sat down, smoothing her full skirt.

"Jason gave me chapter and verse on your battle," Fran told him. "And Mike, I think you were right. Jason hated to lose the chance for the limelight, but his plan was reckless in the extreme in the face of Phil van Zandt's sworn opposition."

He nodded. Catching Tarow's signal, he stood up.

"Folks, we wanted you here this day to see the actual start of construction of the Blue Grouse Tunnel. All of you are friends, some of you are stockholders. In any event, we feel that this initial blast is a turning point in the short history of the Castle Lode, and of Juniper. So I am pleased to introduce Mr. Jason Tarow, president of the Blue Grouse Development Company."

This was right down the little man's alley. He thanked them for their attendance, their participation morally and financially, and gave a brief résumé of what Blue Grouse would do for the region. As he finished, there was a splendid spatter of applause.

Kendall had been sitting with watch in hand. As Tarow finished and glanced at him, Kendall nodded. Tarow walked to the rim of the precipice. He doffed his hat and waved it around his head three times. Peering down, they could see Steve Hradic, Kendall's chief powderman, walk leisurely to the face, shielding his miner's lamp with his hand. Deliberately he lit the fuses. With quick steps he moved away.

There was drama in the moment. A hush fell in the canyon. The warm quiet of the spring afternoon stood still. The long cry drifted up to them: "Fi-i-i-re in-n-n the ho-o-ole!"

Kendell began counting to himself. He knew the fuse lengths, but the wait still seemed interminable. Then came a booming thump. It thrust at the soles of the feet, rapping at the solar plexus. Another-another-another, in quick succession, the rock dust rising, boulders and fragments raining through the canyon. A single chip ticked against the rock barrier, another struck the wood. Then all was silent.

"Ladies and gentlemen, Blue Grouse is begun," Jason Tarow cried.

CHAPTER SIX

Ruth Hagen was sitting next to Kendall at the long dining table. She looked around the room, at the screened windows, the large fireplace at one side, the tables beyond, where the tunnel crew was eating.

"This surprises me a little," she told Kendall.

"The camp crockery and the tin plates and hardware?" he asked. "We're having fun with you. And everyone seems to be enjoying the novelty of drinking a fine Médoc out of tin cups."

"Not that, although it is unusual," she said. "But this room—the sliding windows let in the air and keep out the flies, the kitchen is at one end for convenient serving, and that great fireplace will make this a pleasant place to pass the long winter evenings."

"I've eaten many meals in dining hall and cookshack," Kendall told her. "I tried to put in the best points I had observed. That fireplace will need help from a couple of barrel heaters this winter, but it will make the place more pleasant. Cabin fever is one of our worst enemies in winter in a spot like this. Anything that keeps the men contented is worth the effort."

"You have a good cook," Ruth said. "Of course, he doesn't serve Marsala, Médoc, and tawny port as a regular thing, I presume."

"Hardly," Kendell said, laughing. "Besides, I'm sure the men would prefer the whisky that Jason provided for them as their part of the celebration. Look at them—having the time of their lives."

"I imagine the job will be long enough and dull enough by the day you hole out," Ruth said, "though I hear the monotony of Blue Grouse will be relieved by the feminine touch." She made a slight motion of her head toward Fran Diamond, chatting with Jason Tarow at the head of the table.

"Yes, Lock Graney and I couldn't get along. I asked Jason for a change, so he's sending Fran. She is, he tells me, a first-class accountant and office worker."

"It will be strange, one woman among so many men."

"That's fate—here's a girl with a clear field and no competition, and she's already promised."

"Jason, you mean? I hadn't thought ..." She stopped. She took a sip from her cup of wine. "Mike, what is your honest opinion of Jason?"

Her question took him by surprise. "You know him better than I do, Ruth. But I'll say that he has charm, brains, tenaciousness, and much ability. Look, right now, how he has Long Sam Carlson eating out of his hand. Jason is a true promoter and he loves it. Just as I am a builder. I like him, Ruth."

"Everyone does," she said. "I would hate to see anyone take advantage of him. His dream means too much to Juniper and its people."

"Oh, l think Jason can hold his own in any company," he said.

"Do you?" she asked. She was silent for a time, toying with her wine cup. When she resumed the conversation, it was on less personal subjects.

It was late evening before Jason Tarow's party broke up, with the long drive home still ahead of them. But the success of the initial blast had left everyone in a carefree mood. It was a warm spring night, flooded with moonlight, so the drive over the mountain held few terrors. Kendall went out into the long pale dusk to see them off.

Fran Diamond leaned down from Tarow's buggy. "I'll see you Sunday, Mike. Will my mansion be ready?"

"Complete with gold doorknob and silver grate shaker," he promised. "Are you bringing her, Jason?"

The little man was slightly flushed with wine. "I'll bring her, Mike my boy. Want—wantta check on progress, too. A good start today, Mike. Keep it up. I con-congrashulate you."

He flicked his whiplash across the rumps of the team and the buggy pulled away in a roil of dust, with Tarow leaning forward whooping like Jehu, and Fran clinging to the seat with one hand, the other holding her cartwheel hat. Aaron Hagen pulled out more sedately with Ruth, the girl giving Kendall a smile and a wave of the hand as they passed. The others departed one by one until only Pete Trump and his wife remained.

"Daggone, Mike, I've been trying to get a word with you all afternoon," the sheriff said. "Didn't want to be too public about it. But you ought to know this—we pinned down the fact that the slugs that were fired into the Hagen house could have come from Eddie Lamb's gun. I fired some test shots into an old mattress, and the bullets match the one from the Hagen's exactly, far as I can tell. Can't prove it, o' course, but I'm positive that's the rifle."

"And so..."

"And so, since it couldn't be Eddie, it was likely Claude Lamb. Mike, I'd like to get the boy away from that murdering old hypocrite. He ain't good for Eddie, might get the kid into trouble, if he's Phil van Zandt's man. Will you give the boy a job here?"

"I don't know why not. What can he do?"

"He's young, but he's a top-notch miner, I'll guarantee. He can run a jackhammer, stoper or drifter. He's a fairly good powderman. He knows rock. The boy isn't stupid, Mike. Some people get that idea because he can't talk. But he'll earn every cent of his wages and then some."

"Sounds all right to me. But can you get him to come?"

"Helen can, I'm sure," Trump said. "He'll do anything she asks him."

"That won't be hard, Mr. Kendall," Helen Trump said. "Eddie is afraid of his uncle. The man beats him, I think."

"Ask Jason to bring him, then, when he comes out Sunday. But one thing, Pete. If the boy's presence starts Claude Lamb to hanging around Blue Grouse, I'll have to give Eddie his walking papers."

"I don't think you need to worry. There's a lot more scope for Claude's hell-raising in Juniper than out in the mountains, Eddie or no Eddie," Trump said, grinning. "Thanks, Mike. Be seeing you."

Kendall watched them go, their dust cloud turning opaque as it drifted upward into the fading light.

Tom Hughes, Kendall's tunnel foreman, was a Welshman, grizzled, tough, laconic. A typical hard-rock man. As the bore hammered on into the virgin rock, Hughes proved to be a top man.

"We're getting strung out, Mike," he told Kendall. "It's like all jobs, seems like a man chews away at it forever. Drill your shot holes, put in your V cut or your pyramid cut, maybe some relief holes or trim holes. Pull back the jumbo and the Ingersolls and the hoses, tamp in the giant and blow the face. Muck out rock and haul it away. Then set up the jumbo and do it all over again." He worried a chaw off a battered plug of tobacco. "After a while, a man could do it in his sleep."

"If the guts of Castle Mountain are as tricky as I think they are, you'll have plenty to keep you awake soon," Kendall promised.

"Well, we're making hole and the eagle screams every week," the Welshman said. "Guess a body can't ask much more."

Kendall was not surprised to find that the tunnel gave him a feeling of unease. Nothing critical, but a certain discomfort, a tightening of the stomach, a tendency to look over his shoulder at small noises. A souvenir, he supposed, of Lobchick. But with the tunnel going well, he was happy enough to spend his time in the open, laying out the telephone line to Juniper.

From experience he knew that the perversity of the inanimate was perfectly demonstrated in a mountain telephone line. With this in mind, he put aside the temptation to route the line straight over the crest of the ridge, as the crow would fly. He did angle it across the loop of the supply road, but kept it where a man on snowshoes could reach it during the winter. And snow was early and deep in this altitude.

Irish Murfree cut native pine poles. Kendall picked out a pair of likely young men, Bentz and Skiffen, and taught them how to use a pair of hooks and a safety strap, knowledge that had come to Kendall the hard way in his varied career. He put Tod Skiffen in charge of the crew, gave him men and a team and wagon, pointed at the pile of crossarms and insulators just unloaded from the supply wagons, and said, "Go to it, Tod. She's your pigeon."

Skiffen grinned, hitched up his pants, hung a coil of wire over his shoulder and walked away.

On Saturday afternoon Tom Hughes came out of the tunnel and hailed Kendall, who was walking toward the boiler house.

"Well, I got me wakin' up as you predicted," he said.

"Trouble?" Kendall asked.

"Not bad, but enough. Our last blast opened up a seam. Yon mountain's leaking like a sieve."

"I'll take a look. What's the chance of sealing it off?"

"Good, I would guess. If we can angle in behind it with a stoper drill, we can try forcing grout in under air pressure. That ought to stop 'er. But Mike, it ain't a good sign."

"I've heard a theory that Castle Mountain is just one great sponge, soaked with water," Kendall said, following Hughes into the tunnel. "If they are right, there's plenty of trouble ahead." He walked on, feeling again that uncomfortable crawling of the skin at the plash of water ahead.

They inspected the water seepage, decided on how to plug it, and set the men to it. Hughes walked toward the entrance with Kendall.

"Well, Mike, no hard-rock job ever went as smooth as a maiden's butt for very long," he said. "Guess we'll have to figure 'em out as they come along. There ain't no mining problem a man can't lick, given money, time, men and plenty of guts."

"Right enough, Tom. I hope Jason put enough fat into his estimate to allow for work of this kind."

"Don't worry about Jase. He's been there before. But say, Mike, something else does worry me. I mentioned it to Jason a while back, before you took over. What happens if we hit mineral in this drift?"

"Not much danger, in this formation. But I assume we have mineral rights covering the whole route."

Hughes shook his head. "That's the sticker. This is a old minin' district. Nearly every inch is plastered with some claim. None of 'em this side of the ridge ever amounted to shucks. But a few of 'em ain't run out yet, and Jason could stump his toe thereby. When I told him about it, he said he would take care of it. But I misdoubt that he did."

"What leads you to that, Tom?"

"Well, our tunnel adit is smack in the middle of a claim named the Lightning Bug. It has another year to run before it reverts for re-entry due to lack of development work. O' course, the old boy who filed on it don't intend to do anything with it, but unless Jason has moved since last week, we're legally on another man's ground."

Kendall swore softly. Here was a sore spot of the worst kind. How on earth could Jason Tarow have overlooked it?

"Do you know the locator?" he asked Hughes.

"Yeah, very well. An old prospector named Perley Fahnestock. He lives two-three miles up the crick here, all by his lonesome. Got a prospect up there he's been gopherin' for a couple years or so. It was him told me he still had title to the Lightning Bug."

"Tom, this is important. If van Zandt got hold of this ..."

"I happen to know that Perley likes Jason a hell of a lot better than he does van Zandt. But he's a mighty proud old feller, and being ignored hurts his feelings. I was you, I'd sure check on it."

"Thanks, Tom. I'm going up there right now."

"And take a jug of forty-rod and a paper sack of raisins. The old buzzard loves them two things more'n anything."

A short time later, Kendall made his way up the canyon, with the whisky and the raisins in his pack, and a wallet full of bills. He walked fast, still puzzled at the apparent carelessness of Jason Tarow. It rather worried him.

His resurvey had taken him a mile above the campsite, but beyond that he had never seen the canyon of the Blue Grouse. It was a swift little stream, splashing and gurgling along, dropping over ledges with a tinkling rush of white water. There were deep pools, dark and shaded beneath the banks. Kendall marked them in his mind, vowing to drop a line into one or two of them soon. That splash and whorl beyond the willows—rainbow or cutthroat?

As he followed the faint game trail, he became aware of a muted roar, growing louder as he climbed. Something over two miles above camp, he came around a bend to find the source, a magnificent waterfall, a hundred-foot curtain dropping into a deep pool. The rank vegetation at the base was wet with spray. Kendall paused, charmed by the beauty of the picture. But the practical side of his mind began working on another phase of the scene.

The path turned away from the pool and climbed into the rocky decline beyond. Kendall followed it, drenched with sweat now, pausing to rest a few times. Then the trail broke out of the trees on a sheer slope on the edge of a valley. A lake, its silver surface as sheet-smooth as a mirror, filled most of the bottom. At one side, amid tall trees, stood a gray log cabin.

Kendall walked toward it. One of his questions was answered when he saw, breaking off to the right, a well-defined trail. It headed north toward the spine of the ridge. Undoubtedly it would test the heart and muscles of a mountain goat, but the prospector wouldn't mind it a bit. He would call it a short cut.

"Halloo-oo-oo the house!" Kendall called. Some of these hermits were mighty touchy. But there was no answer.

As he walked closer, Kendall saw on the hill above the white scar of a prospect hole. The pile of waste rock below it was of impressive size. If Kendall had not known the tenacity and persistence of prospectors, he could have marked this as a regular mine, with crew and machinery. But without a doubt Perley Fahnestock had moved every ton of that rock by himself.

"Halloo-oo-oo!" he called again.

Brush crackled. A gnarled chunk of a man with a curling brush of gray whiskers came out of the undergrowth. He was buckling his belt. "Heard ye the first time, but couldn't answer," he said. "Who might ye be?"

"Mike Kendall, from the Blue Grouse tunnel job. You're Mr. Fahnestock?"

"Perley, daggone it." The old man stuck out a hand. "Shake, kid. You look a mite young to be running that spread. But they tell me you're a hard-rock man from away back."

"Thanks, Perley. Tom Hughes asked me to give you his regards, too. Let's get into the shade. I've got a couple things in my pack for you. Tom said you had some preference."

The old man grinned with delight when the pack was opened. He tore open the sack and stuffed a whole handful of raisins into his ample mouth. "Seddown," he mumbled, motioning Kendall to the porch steps. He uncorked the jug, slid an elbow under it, and tilted it up for a long swig.

"Mighty good stuff, mighty good," he vowed, tears standing in his eyes. "Here, young Mike, have one on me!"

Kendall tipped the jug, drank lightly, handed it back. Perley Fahnestock sampled it once more, then drove the cork back in with the heel of his hand. "Save 'er for a rainy day," he explained. "But dang it, it's surprisin' how often it rains this side of the ridge. Now, what axe you want to grind?"

Kendall had an idea he knew his man. Perley Fahnestock wasn't the type you could buck, wheedle, or cajole.

"Perley," he said, "some people think a prospector is like a sheepherder, half loco from living by himself. Well, I've known plenty of prospectors like you, and every one of 'em has been a shrewd and thoughtful person. So I'm not going to beat around any bushes. The Blue Grouse is drilled into a mining claim that belongs to you. There isn't any mineral in the claim. But you could, if you wanted, hold Jason Tarow and his backers up for a nice pile. The question is—would Perley Fahnestock act in that way?"

The old man pointed a gnarled finger at Kendall. "I been fig-gerin' on this. S'pos'n' I told you I wanted one million dollars?"

CHAPTER SEVEN

"A million?" Kendall asked coolly. "Well, then the horse trading would begin."

The old man laughed heartily, slapping his thigh.

"Damn' if I don't like you, Mike Kendall," he said. "But you think I'd block the Blue Grouse for a million, or two million? What would my old friend Tom Hughes and the people of Juniper think of Perley Fahnestock? Hell, I ain't that hard up for beans and bacon yit. Only thing is, I'd like to see the little man squirm some, for being so careless, not takin' up my rights. Dang it, a man likes consideration."

"You're right as rain, Perley," Kendall said seriously. "I don't understand it either. But I'd like to remedy it."

"Horse trade, huh? Well sir, you know as well as I do the Lightning Bug ain't got no more mineral in it than a tombstone. S'pos'n' you make an offer."

"Five hundred dollars for all rights."

"Fifty."

Kendall caught the twinkle in the old man's bright eye.

"Four hundred," he said, falling in with the game.

"Sixty," Perley Fahnestock said.

"Two hundred, and I'm near my limit."

"I'll go ye eighty."

"One hundred dollars, and not a cent less," Kendall said firmly.

"Done with ye!" the prospector said, reaching out a hand like a steel claw. "Let's go inside and sign the papers. And I think she's comin' on for rain. We'd better untie that white mule again."

The cabin was well built, the furniture homemade, but everything neat and shining. At a desk that had once been a packing case, Kendall made out the relinquishment form "... for the sum of one dollar and other valuable considerations, I hereby sell, devise, and relinquish to the Blue Grouse Development Company, its heirs and assigns forever, all right and interest in that particular claim in the Castle Mining District known as the Lightning Bug...."

The prospector read the bill of sale with care. He asked Kendall to change a phrase here and there. "This ain't the first one of these here papers I've signed. Might as well be almighty legal about it while we're at it."

When Fahnestock had signed, Kendall counted out the hundred dollars. The old man folded the bills and shoved them into a pocket of his faded overalls. He uncorked the jug and poured out a double libation.

"Mud in your eye, and confusion to the enemy!" he declared. He downed halt the tumblerful and put the glass firmly on the deal table.

"Just betwixt us, Mike, I was glad to see you come today. The last time I was in Juniper certain parties were showing interest in the Lightning Bug. You know who they are. And if none of you people had come around here, and they asked me to sell, I wouldn't be beholdin' to anybody to hang on. Maybe I might have stalled a few days, though I ain't sure that would be healthy. That feller van Zandt is a tough monkey."

"If he hasn't approached you, you can forget it."

"That so? Well, take a look outen that window, then."

Kendall walked over and pushed aside the scrim curtain. Two men rode into view, down the short-cut trail to the lake's edge. Kendall had seen them—Napper Fegg, a lean, wolfish man with a soiled smile, and the giant, Drag Kryder. They halted in front of the cabin.

"Anybody home?" Kryder called out.

The prospector walked toward the door. "You stay here and back me up. I want to hear their pitch." He walked out.

"Howdy, boys," Kendall heard him say. "What can I do for ye?"

"A big business deal, old-timer," Napper Fegg said, swinging down from his horse. Kendall moved closer to the door, where he could see most of the yard through the hinge opening.

"Business? State your proposition, and be on your way," Perley Fahnestock said belligerently.

"Don't be owly, pardner," Fegg said. "You ain't so proud you hate money?"

"Whose money? Napper, you never had two honest shillings to rub together at a time, less'n some fancy gal give 'em to you. And Drag, you ain't much better."

Kryder grunted. Fegg stood still, one foot on a step.

"Is Phil van Zandt's money spendable, Perley?" he asked.

"Why, shoh, but the Chuckaluck ain't for sale. Why, that mine…"

"That what you call that prospect you're gopherin' in the mountain yander? It'll be a cold winter day before Phil falls for that pig in a poke. No, we want to buy the Lightning Bug."

"Now, them's harsh words for my discovery claim. I tell you, boys, in the whole Castle Lode—but forget that. The Lightning Bug, now. Hell-fire and dangnation, boys. I don't own the Bug no more. If I'da knowed…"

"You sold it, you old fool?" Fegg rasped. "What's the idea, when you knew Phil wanted it?"

"Never said no such to me," the old man said with asperity. "And look out who you're callin' a fool."

With a bound Napper Fegg was up on the porch. He grabbed a handful of the prospector's beard, wrenched it hard.

"Then you better unsell it, you hear? When Phil van Zandt wants something, he wants it. You get me, old-timer?" He gave the beard another twist that sent Fahnestock to his knees.

Kendall stepped out of the door. He caught Fegg's wrist, pulling the man toward him, and clubbed a fist to Fegg's jaw. The man staggered backward, pitched off the stoop to land on his rump in the gravel. He sat looking up dazedly at Kendall.

"You bother Perley again, Fegg, I'll smash you like I would a cockroach," Kendall said. "Kryder, that goes for you as well."

Kryder dropped the reins of his horse. He started toward the steps.

"You want trouble, Fatso?" Kendall asked, bracing himself, wondering what tactics, short of a double-bit axe, might discourage the giant.

Kryder did not slow down. Then a voice spoke behind Kendall.

"I ain't one to be inhospitable, boys. But the fust one comes a step nearer, I'll blow daylight through him with this Sharps. And dang it, if either one of you is on my claim sixty seconds from now, I'll let you have it anyhow. Anybody who would say the Chuckaluck is country rock..."

Kendall glanced over his shoulder at Fahnestock. The old man was cradling a huge Sharps under his arm, looking as if he knew how to use it.

"You ain't heard the last of this, neither of you," Kryder threatened. But he was backing away as he said it. Fegg picked himself up out of the dust, and they moved toward their horses.

Kendall came down the steps as the men mounted. "This doesn't settle our score, Kryder," he said. "Remember, if anything happens to Perley, I'll take care of both of you. Personally."

"You talk to van Zandt," Fegg said, wheeling his horse.

"The day when van Zandt ran the Castle Lode is over," Kendall said. "Remember that, you two. And walk the straight and narrow."

The men rode off up the ridge toward Juniper. When they were out of sight, Perley Fahnestock lowered the Sharps. "Whew!

That was a close one. Remind me, Mike, one day to get a box of ca'tridges for this old baby. Ain't had none since eighty-nine!"

"Why, you old fraud!" Kendall said. "I should have let them pull your fingernails out by the roots until you signed their deed."

"They'd have done it, too," the prospector said. "Glad you got here fust. You want to stay for supper? Rainbow trout, beans, and sourdough bread."

"Sounds great, old-timer, but I've got to get back to camp. Come down and give us your advice now and then, we can use it." He shook hands with the old man and started down the trail.

Kendall made good time downstream, now that he knew the trail. The shadows were lengthening now, and in the shady depths of the canyon the air was almost chill. He walked fast toward camp.

Still, it was well before supper when he turned the last bend. So he was startled to find no signs of activity around the tunnel mouth. The compressor was silent. No mules plodded along with their train of ore cars. Not a man was in sight.

Perturbed, Kendall cut across into the side coulee and up to Bunkhouse Flat. A small crowd of men was gathered on the porch of the office. Two saddle horses were tethered to the rail.

Pete Trump was there. The other was Sprague Laurens, Thelma van Zandt's special interest. Kendall went up the steps.

"What's going on, Pete?" he asked Trump.

"Laurens has a paper, Mike," Trump said grimly. "I had to come and witness that it was served on you."

With an air of triumph Laurens handed a paper to Kendall. It was folded in the narrow voucher style of legal documents. Kendall read it quickly. He refolded it then.

"This is over my head, Pete," he said. "Judge Warner's name is signed to it, so I assume it is legal. But I don't understand how the Queen Mining Company can own the Lightning Bug claim, when we own it. So how can the court enjoin us from working on it?"

"I think you'll find there was a slight slip-up, Kendall," Laurens said. "Jason Tarow intended to get this old claim. But he didn't do so. And van Zandt and I have it."

"This the same claim that was located by one Perley Fahnestock?" Kendall asked. Laurens nodded. Kendall reached in his pocket and drew forth the bill of sale. "Take a look at that, then," he said.

Laurens' face changed color as he read. His hawk face was angry as he finished. Trump took the paper from him.

"What do you think of it, Laurens?" Kendall asked.

"I don't understand. The boys …"

"I lucked out on them. I got there first. What did you and van Zandt do, get an injunction on the strength of a purchase you hadn't made yet? I'd heard van Zandt had the judge in his pocket, but this is about as raw a deal as I've ever come across," Kendall said. He turned to Trump. "And you, Pete? Are you one of van Zandt's puppets too?"

The sheriff shook his head. He handed the bill of sale back to Kendall.

"You should know me better than that, Mike. This injunction is legal, and I had to serve it. But that paper of yours should lift it in a hurry. Damn you, Laurens, for ringing me in on your shady deals."

"Don't blame it on Laurens," Kendall told him. "He's just a pretty boy who picks up crumbs from van Zandt's table. Pete, wait until I change my clothes. I'll ride back to Juniper with you and get this plaster lifted."

Laurens smiled coldly. "I should let you have the trouble for your pains. But Judge Warner left for Helena just after he signed the injunction."

"Well, Laurens, since we are Christians at Blue Grouse and don't work Sundays, I suppose Monday will be just as good."

"Except that the judge said he might be gone for a week," Sprague Laurens said, smiling thinly, that chill smile of his.

"I didn't know that," Pete Trump said. He turned to Tom Hughes. "Tom, do you understand what an injunction is?"

"Not me, Pete," Hughes said.

The sheriff turned to Laurens. "Isn't that a shame? If I had time, I'd explain it, Tom. But since you don't understand it, I ain't sure that I could arrest you for breaking it. Come on, Laurens. Let's get back to town."

"But—but you should have armed men here. Men to see that they don't work," Laurens protested.

"I served the injunction. I doubt if Mr. Kendall will flout the majesty of Judge Warner's court, but I can't stick around to see. There's been an epidemic of horse stealing at the far end of Quartz County." Trump was smiling now.

Laurens was still protesting as they rode away. Trump gave Kendall a wink and a wave of the hand. "I'll have Tarow's lawyer get to work on dissolving this," he said. "Come, Laurens."

"They had me scared," Tom Hughes said to Kendall as they watched the two men ride away.

"Just some more hokery-pokery," Kendall said. "They didn't even wait to see if Fegg and Kryder were successful. You know, Tom, enough of these annoyances will build up into a burden."

"None of 'em will stop the job for long, though. Was I them, Mike, know what I'd do? I'd let you go your sweet way until you had a million or so sunk into this hole in the rock. Then I'd hit you with everything at once, smash the machinery, blow up the tunnel, put you out of business in one stroke. With your money gone, where would you be? Up the crick so fur you'd never get back."

Kendall rubbed his chin thoughtfully. "On that line of reasoning, nothing big would happen before next spring."

"That's the way I'd call it. Keep your guard up, watch for all kinds of deviltry. But I'd bet a month's wages van Zandt won't try for a real knockout until our chins are stuck out farther. Remember, Mike, nearly all of Juniper is on our side."

"I know for a fact that van Zandt would consider the money angle all-important," Kendall said. "If he did anything before spring, it would cost us something, delay our progress, but we'd dig out and get going again. But next spring—that would be another story."

"Yeah, just like I said. Look, Mike, this injunction thing—it's so damn' stupid Sprague Laurens musta thought it up all by himself. Believe me, when van Zandt goes to work, we won't be worryin' about that kind of skeeter bite."

"You could be right, Tom. But in case you're wrong, I want one man by day and two by night, who will do nothing but patrol the job, watching for trouble."

"I'll set it up right away. You want them armed?"

Kendall shook his head. "Too much chance of an accident. Just see that they can yell good and loud if need be. Remember, we can throw a hundred tough hard-rock miners at them on a minute's notice. And the boys would love the chance."

CHAPTER EIGHT

Kendall helped Fran Diamond down from the surrey, catching a flash of trim ankles amid a swirl of frilly petticoats. Laughing, she said, "Mike, it's good to see you. There were times I doubted I would, the way Pete drives this bay team of his."

"They're high steppers, all right," Trump said, getting down from the surrey. "But they're safe enough, I harness-broke 'em myself. Helen, watch it now. There we are. Eddie, bring Miss Diamond's luggage."

They walked past the office to the small log cabin that would house Fran Diamond, a cabin so new the bright chips still lay along the walls.

With a flourish, Kendall handed the girl a key. "Your own private domain, Miss Diamond. And the key to bolt the rude world outside."

She looked at him suspiciously. "Keys usually come in pairs," she said.

He shook his head, reached into his pocket, and brought out the second key. "My villainous plans thwarted so easily," he sighed.

Helen Trump laughed. "Don't give up, Mike. All girls like to thwart villainous plans. It's good practice. Come, Fran, let's inspect your rustic mansion." They went in, Eddie Lamb following with the luggage.

"Where's Jason?" Kendall asked.

"He said to tell you he's greasing wheels. Long Sam Carlson."

ROBERT MCCAIG

"Long Sam likes to know where his money goes. I see you brought Eddie Lamb. How did he like the idea of working here?"

"He was tickled pink," Trump said. "Claude Lamb is crazy as a hoot owl, and getting crazier every day. I think the boy is scared to death of him."

"He'll be safe here. Did you hear any kickback on the injunction deal?"

"I heard Phil van Zandt was fit to be tied," the sheriff said. "Since Fegg and Kryder didn't buy or bluff Perley out of his claim, van Zandt certainly will look the fool when Jason's attorney gets him in court Wednesday. That's when Judge Warner gets back."

"And I take it Phil van Zandt is a very vain man," Kendall said.

"Regular strutting cock. Can't stand to be proved wrong—in anything."

"I don't like that fellow, Pete. He and I are heading for a tangle some day."

"I hope I'm there," the sheriff said. "Of course your crews will be loafing tomorrow?"

"Oh, sure," Kendall told him. "You'll be here to see that we do that?"

"I'm tied up until after Wednesday," Trump told him, straight-faced. "Might drop out here after that."

Kendall suppressed a smile. It was good to have friends.

Fran Diamond and Helen Trump came out of the cabin, Eddie Lamb with them. Kendall pointed out the bunkhouse to Eddie, and the boy shouldered his bedroll and hiked toward it.

"Mike, it's a regular little doll house," Fran Diamond said to Kendall. "I'm going to love living in it."

"Glad you like it," he told her. "I turned the job over to Irish Murfree, and gave him a free hand. What did you think of it, Helen?"

"Perfect in every respect," Helen Trump said. "I'd like to spend the summer out here myself. Pete, hadn't we better be getting back to Juniper? Since you're leaving in the morning?"

They watched the Trump surrey splash across the creek and head up the hill. Kendall turned to Fran Diamond.

"I'm sorry, Fran, if I was the cause of you being exiled out here in the tall timber. You won't find it bad this summer, but when winter comes ..."

"I don't mind a bit," the girl said quickly. "I love the mountains, and in Juniper, well, Jason is so busy anyhow—" she hesitated. "I'm sure we'll get along well, and I know there's plenty of work."

He took her arm and walked back to her cabin with her.

"Not all work, Fran. I've a saddle horse I don't have time to keep in trim. And there are some still, deep holes up the Blue Grouse that look perfect, if you know the difference between a royal coachman and a Parmachene Belle."

She laughed. "My late papa, Lou Diamond, was probably the finest fly fisherman on the eastern slope of the Rockies. He should have been, he fished most of the time he should have tried to earn a living for Ma and us kids. But he did teach me the fine art of angling."

"Good. I'll show you where the old lunkers hang out. Now, I suppose you want to get settled. Had supper? All right, then. I'll see you in the morning."

She paused on the steps of her little cabin. "You're going to ignore the injunction?"

"Of course. Pete understands it was a put-up job. And it will be dissolved Wednesday anyhow. By the way, Fran, by what monumental slip did Jason miss title to the Lightning Bug?"

"You want to say 'I told you so'? You can, Mike. Jason had told Lock Graney to clear up all those titles, the Lightning Bug especially. Lock claims it was an oversight."

"Damned convenient one for van Zandt. But I hope Jason doesn't tie a can to him."

"I don't think he will. You know Jason, the biggest heart in the whole world. Any sob story touches him. Why, do you want Graney left where he is?"

"Pipe lines work both ways, Fran. I might be able to use that fact later."

He left her at the door of the cabin and went over to the main bunkhouse. He found that Eddie Lamb was settled and already making acquaintances. When the boy saw Kendall, he scribbled a note and gave it to Kendall.

"I like it here. If my uncle Claude comes will you make him go away?"

"Sure will, Eddie," he assured the boy. "If he shows up we'll put the run on him quicker'n you can say Edward Lamb."

The boy chuckled, and looked relieved.

Everybody at Blue Grouse liked Eddie, Kendall learned in the next few days. He was a competent workman in any phase of hard-rock work, and he always had a smile. Kendall felt a sense of shame at his own qualms about the tunnel, when he saw the boy going about his tasks with no hint that he had lost his own father in the depths of the Winkin Jack. Yet try as he would, Kendall felt the cold fingers of fear play along his spine every time he went in to the working face.

On Monday, prompt with the shriek of the boilerhouse whistle, Fran Diamond came into Kendall's little office. She was sensibly dressed in dark skirt and plain shirtwaist. Kendall showed her the records, the supplies, and the filing system, the latter in a woeful state of confusion.

"I'll start here," Fran announced. "When I get some order out of this chaos, I'll get out the payroll and the progress report."

"A fine idea," he said. "And Jason tells me he wants you to see about improving the commissary, and cutting costs. A word of warning, Fran. More than one job has gone to hell in a handbasket because the contractor tried to play horse with the men's food and lodging."

"I know what you mean. But I learned long ago that a construction job, like Napoleon's army, marches on its stomach," she said, lining pencils neatly on the desk before her.

Ten days later he joined his telephone crew as they brought the new line into Juniper. They dropped it down the hill and into the alley back of Jason Tarow's office. There Tod Skiffen had mounted the wooden telephone instrument on the wall in Tarow's inner office. Kendall helped Skiffen fish the wires through the porcelain tubes in the wall. He twisted the wires around the binding posts, checked the lightning arrester and the ground wire, and turned to Jason Tarow.

"She's ready, Jason," he told the promoter. "Anything earthshaking you want to say over your line to Blue Grouse?"

Tarow shook his head. He stepped to the instrument, lowered the transmitter, and turned the crank handle gingerly. The bell tinkled and they waited.

Then Tarow's face broke into a smile. "Why Fran, is that you? Can you hear me? ... Oh, it does, eh? ... Yes, I can hear you, yes, yes. Fine to hear your sweet voice .... Yes, he's right here. Hold on a minute."

He stepped back and handed the receiver to Kendall.

"Hello, Fran," he said into the transmitter.

Her voice came clear and strong over the miles of copper wire. "I'm going to put your new toy to work, Mike. When you come out, bring a case of eating tobacco before the boys lynch the sutler. Maybe one of Horseshoe and another of Climax. And some snoose."

"I'll bring it when I come tomorrow. Everything else all right?"

"Still making hole. Is Graney there? I'll read him the report."

The clerk took the receiver gingerly, as if it would bite. He soon forgot his fears in trying to keep up with the stream of data Fran Diamond was dictating to him.

Kendall and Tarow went out into the clerk's office. Kendall jerked his head toward Graney's back.

"Still got him on, eh? Good. Maybe we can use the little snake for our own ends, before we're through."

"I keep thinking, Mike, Lock honestly did forget about that claim," Tarow said.

"And Phil van Zandt will have a change of heart also?"

"Not that, I'm afraid. He spouted off the day we got the injunction lifted, saying there Were a lot of ways to stop a damned hole in the ground. I think half his rage was at Laurens for going to court without having the Fahnestock claim cinched. But he was really ory-eyed, as the ranch hands say."

"Well, that was a mighty weak punch," Kendall said. "I expect that when van Zandt decides to get rough, he'll go the whole hog." He recounted Tom Hughes's theory of delayed action on the part of van Zandt.

Tarow didn't laugh it off. "Mighty logical, knowing van Zandt's character," he said. "Not that I would relax my vigilance, Mike, but I do think the man will wait until his blows count to do anything drastic. Except for you, Mike—I think he will make a target of you any time."

"I've stuck my neck out before," Kendall said lightly.

"I mean it, Mike. I want you to be on guard every minute. Think of what would happen to the job if you were hurt—or killed."

"Even if I'm not Big Morley Kendall?"

"Skiddoo to that! You're as good as Morley any day."

"Thanks, Jason. See you in the morning," Kendall said. He knew that what Tarow had said wasn't true, but it gave him a pleasant glow just the same.

The maid at the Hagen's ushered Kendall into the parlor and left to find Ruth. He was looking through the latest issue of *McClure's* when she entered. Prettier than ever, he thought, coming to his feet.

"Why Mike, how nice!" she exclaimed, holding out her hand.

"How long since I've seen you—months, weeks?" he asked.

"Merely days," she said, freeing her hand from his. "Are you in town for any length of time?"

"Just tonight," he told her. "Long enough to rubber at the bright lights of Juniper, have a leisurely dinner at the Elkhorn, and perhaps a drive in the cool of the evening, if you're not otherwise occupied."

"I'm foot-loose and fancy-free at the moment. And your program sounds ever so inviting," she said without coyness. "If your patience, good sir, will extend to the necessary time to make myself beautiful."

"You look very lovely as you are," he said, and meant it.

"I'll take only a half hour, then," she said with a smile, and hurried upstairs.

A few minutes later Aaron Hagen came home. He walked into the parlor, hand outstretched.

"Good to see you, young Kendall," he said, paralyzing Kendall's hand in the grip developed by years of swinging a single jack. "But you didn't come to see me, I'll wager."

"It is a pleasure, sir. But I'm squiring your daughter to dinner at the Elkhorn."

Hagen dropped heavily into a Morris chair. "Good for you, son. It's pretty dull for Ruth, with her mother ailing. Jason does his best to cheer her up, but he's a busy man." He tinkled the call bell.

When the maid had brought whisky, soda and glasses and scooted out of the room, Hagen mixed a drink for Kendall. With his own drink in hand, he leaned back.

"Tell me, Mike, how does the work go?"

"Fair enough," Kendall said. "Fran Diamond just turned the figures on progress over to Graney over our new telephone line. You'll be able to follow it now from day to day."

"That will help," Hagen said, frowning. He studied his drink. "When do you say, Mike, you'll finish the tunnel?"

"That's a tough one, Mr. Hagen. So many things can happen. We're hoping to average two hundred feet a week, and are beating that a little so far. But that is in perfect ground, no water to speak of, no timbering. God knows how we might be slowed down if we hit trouble. I'll just say this—we won't hole out before May of next year, but we will almost certainly be through by September."

There was deep worry on the face of the mineowner. "I had hoped it might be sooner," he said. "Mike, those clever, damnably expensive, voracious pigs of steam pumps at the Case Ace are busting me up in business. We're not much more than breaking even right now. Worse, the water is slowly rising in spite of the pumps. Our main pay lead may be submerged by the end of the year. Which means closing down."

"The seepage may slacken after the spring runoff is over."

"We hope so. For if we have to shut down, once flooded it will cost half a million to reopen the Ace, even if Blue Grouse is a success. You know what flooding does to a mine. And frankly, Mike, between slim pickings and what I have sunk in Blue Grouse, I'm on the ragged edge of disaster."

"We're doing what we can, Mr. Hagen," Kendall said. We're running two shifts, and we've got the latest and best equipment, including the Rand Giant drill. The actual work at the face just won't go any faster."

"Even with more equipment? More men?"

Kendall shook his head. "Some improvements in the next few days may help a little. I picked up a Leffel water turbine, a hundred-horse job. We'll mount it at the waterfall above camp and run an alternating current generator with it. We'll bring the power to the tunnel and the camp, with a wire line."

"Lights will help, but beyond that …"

"I've also found a big electric-driven blower. We'll bring air clear to the face with canvas pipe. After a blast we'll blow the nitro fumes out in a hurry, give the muckers fresh air. We'll be able to resume work as soon as the sound of each blast has died away. And I'm mounting arc lights around the working area for the night shift."

"Anything that will speed things up," the mineowner said, a note of desperation in his voice.

"We'll do everything, sir, to keep the Ace ..."

Hagen put a finger to his lips. "Here comes Ruth. Not a word of this to her, young Kendall, or I'll pulverize you."

Kendall smiled. He turned to watch Ruth come down the stairs.

CHAPTER NINE

I t was warm in the dining room of the Elkhorn Hotel. Kendall suggested an ice for dessert at the end of the excellent meal. The waiter had just brought it when Phil van Zandt walked over to their table. The mineowner was dressed in a light summer suit, his white shirt tall of collar, his tie a foulard. The man's face was flushed.

"A warm evening, isn't it, Miss Hagen?" he said to Ruth.

"For the time of year, not unusual," she said coolly.

"A scorcher, though," he persisted. He loked at Kendall. "What brings you to Juniper, Kendall? A fling at the fleshpots? Camp life has palled on you rather quickly."

"It has its drawbacks," Kendall said. "The impossibility of dining in such charming company, for instance."

Van Zandt's eyebrows went up. "Why, you have the lovely Fran at your beck and call. Or isn't she your type?"

"Fran Diamond is Mr. Tarow's fiancée, Phil," Ruth reminded him. "She is not at Blue Grouse to entertain. She is a lady."

"A lady!" van Zandt said. "That's a good one. Fran Diamond came out of the Rabbit Patch beyond Sonoma Street, and everyone knows it. Her mother was ..."

Kendall came to his feet. "Enough of that, van Zandt. Miss Diamond is a friend, and so is Miss Hagen. I don't like scenes, so I'll not ask you to apologize. Just go about your business now without further loud talk."

"Getting mighty big for your boots, Kendall," van Zandt said. His meaty face was dark with anger. He leaned closer to

Kendall. "You know, boy, I think I'm going to have to have you taken care of."

"By Fegg, or Kryder, or some other of your bully boys?"

"Perhaps. When I order it, the method or the man will have no further meaning for you. You'll be gone. You know, the more I think of it, the better I like it. If I eliminate you and Jason Tarow, the tunnel will stop forever."

Kendall stared at the man, realizing that van Zandt was being completely serious. He would have to be, Kendall thought. There is no humor in this monumental egotist.

Before Kendall could answer, Ruth spoke in a voice flat with contempt. "Perhaps Sprague Laurens would do murder for you, Phil. I understand that he takes care of other matters for you to the satisfaction of all concerned."

"Why, you little bitch!" van Zandt exclaimed. His hand went up.

Kendall came around the table. His hip brushed it, making china and glassware rattle. He spun a chair aside and hooked a fist into the mineowner's belly. Van Zandt grunted, toppling forward. Kendall sledged right and left into the beefy face. A thin spray of blood, startlingly crimson, stained the snowy tablecloth. Van Zandt sagged, his eyes glassy.

There was movement behind Kendall. He felt his arms seized, found a husky waiter on each side of him. He did not struggle.

Slowly van Zandt straightened. He mopped at his face with a handkerchief. The long dining room was hushed in expectant silence. Even the clatter from the kitchen was stilled.

With deliberate movements, van Zandt stuffed the stained handkerchief into his coat pocket. He came toward Kendall. Kendall felt the hands on his arms tighten. He saw the face of the mineowner twist with the ferocity of his anger. Then van Zandt shifted his feet and swung a fist at Kendall's face with all the power in his big frame.

A man grows up in the construction camps. He learns the tricks of fist and foot, the knee to the groin and the gouge of the eye—that is, he does if he wants to weather the storm and live through brawls and clems and minor insurrections. These answers Kendall knew. He used his captors as part of his defense.

He leaned back against them, bringing his right knee up to his chest. He drove his foot like a piston, the heel catching van Zandt in the breastbone. With a croak of expelled air, the mineowner hurtled backward. He caromed from a chair, into a table, and went down with it in a crashing crescendo of dishes and silver.

Kendall didn't turn his head. "Get your hands off me," he said.

"But the boss ..." one of them began.

Kendall smashed an elbow into the man on the right, felt him fall away. Spinning, he chopped the other under the ear with the stiffened edge of his hand. The man caved, his knees buckling.

Kendall stood over van Zandt. He wrenched the big man to his feet.

"Never let me hear you loose that filthy tongue of yours in the presence of a lady again, van Zandt," he said.

The man brushed futilely at his drabbled coat.

"I'll have you killed for this," he said savagely.

"I'm not worried about any of your hired men," Kendall told him, "nor you either. So get this, van Zandt. It's open season on you or any of your men, across the ridge. Tell that to Fegg, and Kryder, and Laurens, and especially Claude Lamb. If they come anywhere near Blue Grouse, they'll never go home again."

Van Zandt, holding his handkerchief anew to his bleeding face, tried to stare Kendall down. When it didn't work, he turned on his heel and strode through the dining room. He ignored the amused or disturbed or frightened stares of the diners. The outer door slammed behind him.

"Ready to go, Ruth?" Kendall asked, rubbing the knuckles of his bruised hand.

Without a word she stood up, folding her light stole over her arm. She waited while he paid the cashier and retrieved his straw boater from the rack. He offered her his arm but she did not seem to see it.

Outside in the warm stillness of the evening air, she said, "I—I'm not in any mood for riding, Mike. Would you take me home, please?"

He was hurt by her attitude. He did not especially blame her, for he had brought a public scene down around her. It was no way to impress a well bred girl like Ruth. On the other hand, no man could stand for van Zandt's slurs of Fran Diamond and Ruth herself.

He helped the girl into the rented buggy and drove up the hill.

Beyond the houses, the road in the long evening shadow was a dim tunnel through the trees. The sky above was still bright blue, though streaked with the changing rhythm of sunset colors. The air was touched now with a faint coolness redolent of pine and warm grass, and it was losing the flat smell of the day's drifting dust. Through the dimness of the woods the team moved with easy walk, unhurried and content.

"Stop here," Ruth said suddenly, touching his arm.

He pulled the team off the road into a little glade and halted them. He looked down at the girl.

He caught the glint of tears in her eyes. "Can you forgive me, Ruth?" he asked.

Her head came up in surprise. "Forgive you? Mike, I wouldn't blame you if you never spoke to me again. It was awful of me, Mike. I caused a rare scene in the most public place in Juniper—I put you in a position where you had to defend me with Phil van Zandt. I can't ask you ..."

He interrupted her with a shout of laughter that made the horses flinch and shy with a jingle of harness chains. He grasped her arms, turning her toward him.

"Ruthie, you're a jewel! I was just trying to get up enough nerve to apologize to you for mixing you up in my fight. Don't blame yourself, my dear. I was spoiling for a few licks at that pompous hyena. And he asked for it. Am I forgiven?"

"Of course," Ruth said, smiling now. "But if I hadn't goaded Phil the way I did, he might not have started anything. But he made me so d-damned mad!"

"I take it you don't have much use for Thelma van Zandt—or for Sprague Laurens," he said.

"That kind of people are not good for Juniper," she said in all seriousness. "Mike, Juniper has fine people, barring some of the trash Phil van Zandt hires for the Queen o' Hearts. And most of those would be good citizens if they were let be. If the whole rotten van Zandt household left this town, the town would be greatly improved by it."

"You don't mince words, Ruth," he said, "now or then."

"A girl learns them, Mike," she said, settling back in the buggy seat. "A mining camp isn't a finishing school for young ladies, but it is a liberal education on other lines. Life in one has taught me to recognize a rotten scoundrel like Phil van Zandt. I could only wish that his threats to you and Jason were empty ones, but I'm afraid he means them. Jason, of course, just laughs them off."

"You see Jason a good deal?" Kendall asked.

"Of course," she said, a little surprised. "He comes to see Dad two or three times a week. He's a dear little man, Mike. So good, so well meaning, so wrapped up in the future of the town and its people. I will hate anyone who hurts Jason."

"I like him," Kendall said. "He's a good friend. I feel a little guilty in being the cause of Fran Diamond being away from him. I suppose I could have coped with Graney."

"Oh, no, Mike," she said hurriedly. "It is much better the way it is. Jason is using Lock for his own purposes—I think Graney is one way to keep the enemy camp well misinformed."

"That's true, I know. But she is engaged to Jason."

"He's bearing up," she said tersely. "And it must be more pleasant for you—with a pretty girl in camp, I mean."

Perversely, wanting to annoy her, he said, "She's a grand girl. We've done some trout fishing together, she's an expert. She rides like a whirlwind, she has a lovely singing voice, and on the practical side, her office runs like clockwork with never a hitch. She keeps the cooks in line, the grub is clean and tasty. The men are fond of her. Come to think of it, Graney couldn't possibly take her place."

"Not such a paragon as you describe," Ruth said, laughing. "And Lock Graney is almost certainly trying to sell us out. I have some backstairs gossip, which I hate, but it has Lock a frequent visitor at the van Zandt house. And late at night."

"We might be able to use that fact," Kendall said. "Unless he is attracted there for other than business reasons."

"The magnificent Thelma? She wouldn't waste her charms on such as Lock Graney. Let's use the man, Mike, if we can. I'm ready to scratch and kick and gouge for Daddy's sake, with the Case Ace in danger."

"You know about the status of the Ace, then?" he asked.

"Of course," she said with a touch of scorn. "Men always think they are pulling the wool over the eyes of their women-folk. But Mother and I have known for a long time that the mine was in bad trouble. To keep from worrying Dad, we let him go on thinking he had us fooled. We keep our own worries to ourselves."

Kendall shook his head, his glance admiring. "The devious-ness of the female of the species passes all male understanding," he said.

❧   ❧   ❧

Before he pulled out for Blue Grouse the next day he had a long conference with Jason Tarow. Among other things, the little man complimented him on the new telephone line.

"You were right, Mike. It will save us a good deal of money. Already this morning Fran has given me the progress figures for yesterday—you want to see them? Not bad, eh? And she read off an order Tom Hughes wanted, it will be on the supply wagon tomorrow. I must compliment you, Mike."

"You've got to use every modern method you can, Jason, in this day of rising costs," Kendall said. "Look at them—eight dollars a day for team and driver. A decent suit of clothes sets a man back fifteen cartwheels. Three dollars, it costs for a pair of shoes, three fifty for a good derby hat. I tell you, Jason, a man has to cut corners everywhere he can."

They discussed other phases of the job, disposing of several details. When they finished, Kendall folded his notes and shoved them into an inside pocket. He leaned back in his chair.

"I suppose you heard what happened last night," he said.

"I heard," Tarow said, frowning. "And I'm not pleased about it, Mike. You might have avoided a public brawl when you were in the company of a lady like Ruth."

The little man's smug disapproval rubbed Kendall the wrong way.

"I acted according to my lights, when van Zandt tried to bully me," he said. "And I think, Jason, this is between me and Ruth. I'm not in the notion of having you censoring my private morals. You stick to your last, I'll stick to mine."

"Don't get huffy, Mike," Tarow said placatingly. "I was only looking at the impression it must have made on Ruth."

"Ruth is a big girl now, Jason," Kendall said. "She is capable of her own decisions when they are needed. We understand each other. You have neither invitation nor right to butt into Ruth's affairs."

Tarow looked at him, his face flushed with anger. "You're being rather perverse about this, Mike. I was only ..."

"Let's forget it," Kendall said curtly. "If you want the truth, I should have broken van Zandt's neck right there. I had a good excuse in what he said to Ruth and about Fran Diamond. That man is as mean as a prairie rattler. But he gets away with it—even the waiters at the hotel were helping him."

"They had to. He has a half interest in the Elkhorn," Tarow said. "Better watch that man, Mike. He's dangerous, damned dangerous."

"Remember what I told you about Tom Hughes's theory? That van Zandt would not strike until we had sunk most of our wad into the tunnel? Did you give that any more thought?"

"Tell Tom it's more than a theory," Tarow said, frowning. "I got my initial financing without trouble, with certain payments to come in at regular intervals—a minimum amount to build the tunnel. But I've made some recent inquiries. Van Zandt carries weight in mining and banking circles. He's crowded my backers so that beyond the promised sums, they won't go a single step. From now on, Mike, you've got to keep a tight rein on costs. And we'd all better pray that we don't hit bad ground, or water, or have labor trouble. Van Zandt will be waiting to kick us in the face."

"You can count on all of us across the ridge," Kendall told him. He stood up. "Time to be getting back."

Tarow stood up also. He came around the desk. He put out a hand.

"Mike, forgive my temper a few minutes ago. Because Ruth is my very good friend, I was oversolicitous of her feelings. As you pointed out, it is actually none of my business. Accept my apology."

Kendall shook the promoter's hand. "No offense taken, Jason. I'm edgy too. Van Zandt would make a saint owly."

"That he would, Mike. Give my very best to Fran, will you?"

"Of course. And drop over when you can," Kendall said. He went through the outer office. Lock Graney was suddenly very busy at his high desk. Kendall crossed the sidewalk and untied the rangy saddler he was riding. He struck out for Blue Grouse at a high lope.

CHAPTER TEN

A fter the one scare about bad ground, the Blue Grouse job settled down to monotonous routine through the long summer days and the cool, velvet nights. Kendall left the supervision of the tunnel to Tom Hughes, while he superintended the placement of his water turbine and generator at the falls. With Tod Skiffen and a crew of men, he built a line at eleven hundred volts to the tunnel and the camp. After they turned the water into the flume, there was a day or two of trouble, then the machinery began to function, and they had all the electric power they needed—lights for the camp, water pumped to the kitchen, and big arc lights to illuminate the working area at night.

They ran a circuit into the drift, with a line of electrics each twenty feet along the ceiling. Skiffen and Irish Murfree built a stand to hold a bank of lights near the working face. And along the roof of the tunnel they ran a canvas pipe a foot in diameter, from the electric blower mounted near the entrance, clear to the face. The work speeded up, for with plenty of clean fresh air for the miners, and the clearing of the face of nitroglycerine fumes in only a few minutes after a blast, the cycle of work was much shorter.

So day after day, night after night, it was drill and load, move the jumbo back and secure, light the fuses and wait, counting the jar of each shot in case of misfire. Then blow out the fumes, muck the broken rock into the little cars and haul it away with the patient mules. The damp gray rock from the tunnel piled higher and higher on the dump. And the wound in the heart of Castle Mountain deepened nearly two hundred feet each week.

At Kendall's insistence, the two shifts of the Blue Grouse job operated only six days a week. The custom in the hard-rock country was a straight seven-day week.

"I've got figures to prove my point," he told Jason Tarow. "You have less labor trouble, greater total production, more satisfied crews, if you work six days instead of seven. I don't know just why. But both Morley and I have become convinced of it."

"All right, then," Tarow said. "It's your responsibility, Mike, though Aaron Hagen is getting as restless as a pinto pony in fly time. I think his pumping costs are eating him out of house and home."

This was on one of the promoter's infrequent visits to Blue Grouse. Kendall wondered a little at the man's staying away, though it could be ascribed to the fact that Kendall and Fran Diamond were in constant touch with the Juniper office over the telephone line.

Kendall suspected that Fran felt this neglect keenly at times, though she made no comment. She went cheerfully about her work and did it well. Kendall made it a point to take her fishing with him or riding over the mountain trails when he had a chance to get away. More often he would see her head out alone, on her saddler, or on foot with rod and creel, always coming back from a fishing trip with a fine mess of rainbow or cutthroat trout. She grew slim and wiry and dark-tanned as any Indian as the summer progressed.

Tarow called on the telephone the last day of August.

"I'm coming out tomorrow, and I'll have a visitor with me," he told Kendall.

"We'll roll out the red carpet, and kill the old red rooster," Kendall assured him. "Who's coming?"

"Wait and see," Tarow said with a chuckle audible over the hum of the line.

The next day Kendall stayed around camp, taking the opportunity to catch up on some of his engineering data and drafting. In midmorning Fran Diamond came in, dressed in the boy's shirt and denim trousers she often wore around the job. She tossed her time book on the desk.

"All present and accounted for," she said. "Mike, I'm going to ride down to the Clift ranch. They sent word they had some extra eggs and milk we could get. Cookie wants to get it."

"Good enough. But aren't you going to wait for Jason?"

She gave him an odd look. "I'll be back before he leaves. He doesn't put himself out very much to visit with me. You keep him entertained, Mike."

"I'm not engaged to him," Kendall said, laughing.

"Sometimes I wonder if I am," she replied grimly.

When Tarow's buggy clattered over the log bridge and into camp, Kendall saw with a lift of pleasant surprise that the visitor was Ruth Hagen. He handed her down from the buggy with an air. She was cool and lovely despite the hot drive, fresh in a flowery dress with great puffed sleeves, and a swirling cartwheel of a hat. She opened her parasol against the sun, giving him her other hand.

"Mike, how nice to see you," she said. "You look well, but thin."

"Heat and hard work," he told her. "How are you, Jason? Oh, Billy! Come and take care of these horses."

As the stableman hurried up, the two men and Ruth walked toward the shaded porch of the office.

"You may feel flattered, Mike, my boy," Tarow said. "Ruth is here on your account. She says since you never come to Juniper, she must perforce come to Blue Grouse."

"That's the truth, Mike," she said, giving him a clear direct look without coquetry. "I thought you were turning into a hermit."

"I am remiss, my dear. But forgive me. Out here we have all the burdens of the world on our shoulders. Last month it was water, last week a forest fire that we fought for two days until that rain put the kibosh on it. Today it's a shortage of milk and eggs."

"And tomorrow?" she asked.

He shrugged. "Who knows? But it's never monotonous, I assure you."

In the cool office, Kendall placed chairs for them. The cook, in clean white apron, came running from the cook-shack with a big pitcher of iced lemonade. Kendall filled the glasses.

"Where's Fran?" Tarow asked.

"Gone after those provisions I mentioned earlier. Down to the Clift ranch. She should be back soon," Kendall said.

"I want to talk to her, Mike," the little man said, frowning. "And you too. What about these reports of yours? Are they true?"

The genuine doubt in his voice hit Kendall like a dash of cold water. He stared at Tarow, fighting down a sudden anger.

"That's a hell of a thing—pardon me, Ruth—for you to say," he said. "None of us operate that way, and you know it. Jason, are you trying to be deliberately insulting?"

"No, no, Mike. I'm sorry. I put it badly. But I'm worried about the job. Long Sam Carlson is sick in the hospital in Helena, Fred Lipscomb, the banker, is jittery about Bryan and free silver, and Phil van Zandt is carrying on a whispering campaign about our Luscon Syndicate. Mike, I'm fighting the mulligrubs. Pat me on the back, tell me I'm an idiot, do something."

Kendall stood up. "I know just the medicine for you—a trip into the bowels of Castle Mountain. Nice and cool in there, too."

"I want to go too," Ruth Hagen said.

"In that pretty dress and those fragile shoes? Ruth, you couldn't ..." he began.

Steps crossed the porch and Fran Diamond came into the office. She drew back a little when she saw Ruth. The ride in the sun had left her hot and dusty, her shirt was damp with sweat, and her short curly hair was tousled by the wind.

"Hello, Jason, Ruth," she said. "Mike, I got the supplies. Clift was glad of the sale, he says we can have more until winter closes in. Now will you excuse me? I've got to clean up."

Kendall glanced at Ruth. She was smiling sweetly at the other girl, secure in her daintiness and charm. The air of minor triumph, Kendall supposed, was natural enough, nor in reversed circumstances did he doubt that Fran would wear the same smile. But some perverse whim to help the underdog moved him.

"Just a minute, Fran," he said. "Ruth, do you really want to tour the tunnel?"

"Of course. I've been in Daddy's mine many times. I'm not frightened of the underground."

"Good enough, then. But you can't go in that get-up. Fran, take her over to your place, fix her up in some practical clothes, such as you are wearing. Scoot, now. Jason and I have business."

The two girls went out, Ruth a little bewildered at the turn of events, Fran smiling a little as she closed the screen softly behind her. When they were gone, Kendall turned to the promoter.

"Jason, what brought on this wild hair that's bothering you?"

"I don't know, Mike," Tarow said despairingly. "All the things I told you put the chills up my spine. Then Lock said maybe the tunnel…"

"I thought we'd spot the fine Italian hand of Lock Graney in this mess. Jason, you know he's van Zandt's spy?"

"I'm not sure, Mike. I'm not sure of anything. How could you prove such a thing?"

"He has access to the reports every day. Then here's what we'll do. …" Quickly Kendall outlined the devious plan he had contrived. When he finished Tarow was smiling again. Kendall knew his man.

"That'll pin his hide to the wall all right, if he's guilty," Tarow said. "When would you try it?"

"Not until after snowfall. Some miner might give it away," Kendall said. "I'll let you know. Here are the girls now."

Fran Diamond was much more at ease when she entered. She had washed and donned a clean blouse, had combed her curly hair into a gleaming cap. She winked at Kendall and tipped her head toward Ruth.

Ruth Hagen too was in shirt and levis and boots. Her long hair had been drawn straight back and pinned in a chignon. It made the planes of her face harsher, but more full of character. She was a trifle taller and heavier than Fran, so the borrowed clothes fitted tightly, the denim of the trousers stretched tight across her thighs, the shirt taut against the thrust of her fine breasts. Yet she was a mountain girl. There was no roll of excess flesh around her slim waist, and her belly was as flat and trim as Fran Diamond's.

"Mike, you beast, I feel positively indecent in this rig," she said.

"You look charming, though," Kendall told her. "And it's very practical around the work, as Fran can testify. Shall we go?"

As they walked along the path toward the rim of the coulee which dropped down to the boilerhouse, Kendall heard Tarow say, "You needn't feel self-conscious, Ruth, my dear. The first man who looks sideways at you will be fired on the spot."

"Not that, Jason," Ruth replied. "It's my lookout. I realize that I may not look like a lady in this outfit. But the men can't be blamed for observing that I'm certainly a woman!"

"Darn it, Mike, she's a good sport!" Fran Diamond whispered. "You treed her, you double-dyed, conniving devil."

"On top of that, I think our fireworks have backfired," he said. "A woman in all those flounces and furbelows and jupons and such is pretty but deceptive. But what's in those clothes ahead of us is all Ruth Hagen. Jason is certainly attentive."

"I don't blame him—for the moment," she said. "But he'd better not lick his chops with anticipation. I'll bring his balloon down to earth in a hurry, just you wait."

A string of ore cars waited at the adit. A solemn white mule was hitched to the head end, its reins held by a taciturn Missourian whose whiskery cheek bulged with an enormous chaw of tobacco. His eyes bugged out when he saw the girls in men's clothing. Hurriedly he picked up the reins, looking steadfastly forward. They climbed into the front car and the Missourian clucked to the mule.

By now the tunnel had penetrated nearly half a mile into the raw rock. The cars clanked interminably down the echoing tunnel, the mule keeping a steady unhurried pace. Above them, moisture gleamed on the roof in the yellow light of the electrics. Beside the track a runnel of black water flowed outward. The round snake of the ventilating duct wound along with them, distended with its charge of air. Now and then the smeared design of a leak spat moisture cold on their faces.

Men were working in the stronger light of the massed bulbs, shoveling broken rock into the little cars. The face loomed beyond, with men setting up the jumbo to drill the next round of shot and cut holes. The Missourian halted his mule.

"End o' the line, folks," he said. He shot tobacco juice against the wall, clambered down and unhooked the mule. He turned the animal and hitched it to the outer end of the loaded string.

Kendall took Ruth's arm, helping her over the jumble of rock. He saw her head go back as she sniffed the air.

"Nitro fumes, Ruth," he told her. "Much worse than black powder. Until we got our blower rigged up, everybody worked with a fierce headache most of the time. Watch your step, now. There we are. Tom, how's it going?"

At the sight of the two girls, the foreman's grizzled face was a picture of surprise. Recovering, he swept off his miner's cap. "Howdy, ladies. Never expected to see two pretty girls in the depths of Castle Mountain. Mike, she's going well enough."

"Fine. Still no trouble with water, I see. Let's hope that keeps up."

"Mr. Hughes, how far are we under the mountain?" Ruth Hagen asked. "I've been down in the Case Ace many times, but it doesn't have the eerie feeling I get in this drift."

"The crosscuts, mayhap, give a feeling of room," Hughes said. "And there *is* more rock over your pretty head, miss. Something like three thousand feet of it, right here. When we get in a mile and a half, there will be six thousand feet of solid rock on the top of us."

Fran Diamond shivered a little. "Too much for me. But Mike, what I want to know is how you expect to tap the water. Couldn't you just keep going in solid rock without knowing it?"

"That's Mike's job, Fran," Jason Tarow said. "He's an expert mining surveyor, among his many talents. We have very accurate underground maps of the Case Ace workings—would that we could say the same for the Winkin Jack. Several years ago, Ruth's father mined a rich vein that ran almost due south. Finally the pay petered out and the level was abandoned. That's where we plan to have our drift—this one—tap the Case Ace workings."

"But suppose he misses such a small target?" she insisted.

"That's what I'm getting paid for, Fran," Kendall told her. "I have to be right, or I'll drown all of us." Even as he said it, he felt the cold fear tingle at the nape of his neck. "When we get close, we'll set off a large blast, to make an opening that will drain the water out of the lode through our tunnel. If it's trapped water, it will drain out eventually, but if it's an underground river, nobody will actually sec the end of this tunnel, ever."

He went forward with Tom Hughes to discuss the next round, the placement of the cut and trim holes. When he came back he said, "Seen enough? Ready to go back?"

They rode back toward the portal behind a red mule driven by a young man named Bentz. The trip seemed shorter, the loaded cars rolling more easily and quietly than the empties.

Fran Diamond was still thoughtful. "Mike, if you tap the water in the lower level of the Case Ace, will that drain the whole Castle Lode?"

"We hope so, Fran. If not, Jason and his Luscon Syndicate have permission to run a crosscut from the Jack into the Ace."

"But Phil van Zandt will benefit, though he hasn't put in a red cent," she protested.

"That's right," Jason Tarow said. "For the Queen is almost certain to experience flooding sooner or later, without the relief of this tunnel. But I suppose we can put up with that, if our mines are producing again."

"Daddy said nobody can get a word out of Phil's miners," Ruth said.

"They're as close-mouthed as clams," Tarow said. "They're picked men—men with criminal records, or burdened with debt, or in some scrape or other. A lovely collection of misfits, ruffians, and general bad hats. Many of them the sweepings of Butte's back alleys. They have nothing for the decent people of Juniper but the back of their hands. I don't trust a mother's son of them."

The distant patch of daylight grew larger. Suddenly they were out in the open, blinking at the intensity of the sunlight. The little train clanked over switch points and stopped. As they clambered from their car, Missouri drove past inbound, the nipper waving a hand at them from the front car, bristling with his fresh steel for the pounding Ingersolls.

"That sun feels good," Ruth said as they climbed the slope toward Bunkhouse Flat.

"It *is* cold in the tunnel," Kendall admitted, "but it never changes. It will still be very nearly the same temperature as now when it is forty below this winter. Remember that, Ruth."

"And come to crawl into it? Mike, when it is forty below, I will be curled up with a book alongside a sizzling steam radiator. I'll think of you in your old tunnel then."

When Ruth drove off with Tarow, an hour later, her feminine self again, Fran Diamond turned to Kendall.

"Mike, why can't I be like that?" she asked.

"Like what?"

"Like Ruth—calm and ladylike, poised in any situation. Plenty of beautiful clothes, a good education, a wealthy family."

"Ruth's mother is a semi-invalid," Kendall pointed out. "And if Blue Grouse fails, her father is flat broke. She knows it, too."

"That makes me madder yet—she's such a good sport on top of everything else. I wouldn't have taken that clothes business like she did. I'd have been spitting like a wet cat."

"I doubt that. I don't know why you low-rate yourself. You're pretty, forthright, you face up to any situation. As for wealth, as Mrs. Jason Tarow, you'll ride in a swank carriage in finery as well as any Ruth Hagen will ever own."

"If I ever become Mrs. Jason Tarow," she said morosely, and head lowered, she hurried away toward her own cabin.

CHAPTER ELEVEN

The summer slid away as the swift mountain summers do. Of a sudden the leaves of the poplars were quivering golden discs, then they dropped away, to rattle in the cold fall wind. The edge of Blue Grouse Creek, in the early mornings, was rimed with ice. Before long it would be bridged over. The great ricks of wood the choppers had cut and mounded in late summer began to show indentations as sticks of firewood were needed to feed the bunkhouse stoves.

Kendall was satisfied with his preparations as winter came on. The compressed air lines were boxed in with insulation of hay, the storeroom was piled high with cased and smoked food, the powderhouse was chock full of dynamite and blasting powder. The crews were now shaken down, with the drifters and the sea lawyers and the incompetents weeded out. On occasion a man or two would get cabin fever, or suffer some fancied insult, and pull the pin, heading for the fleshpots of Juniper on foot or supply sleigh. But the core of steady workmen stayed on, making tunnel, their wages accumulating as a credit on Fran Diamond's payroll ledger.

So it was a taut, shipshape job when a snowstorm in November blocked the supply road solid, leaving the telephone line the only link between Blue Grouse and Juniper. It would be days before anyone could get in or out of the camp.

Kendall handed Fran Diamond a sheet of notepaper. "You can telephone this progress report to Lock Graney, Fran," he said.

She read it, looked at it again. She turned startled eyes to Kendall. "But Mike, is this right? Only half the footage they made the day before? Why, we haven't been that short since the compressor breakdown in September."

"It's time we slowed down, then," he said, smiling.

She shook her head dubiously and reached for the telephone.

"It doesn't mean what it says, Fran," he told her then. "Jason knows the code. But Lock Graney and his boss will think we're slowed down to a snail's pace."

"So they won't be in so much of a hurry to ruin us."

"Exactly. We're buying time. If we can get through the winter without serious interference from van Zandt, he might find it hard to do us injury by spring. We'll be too far along."

"Are you sure Lock Graney is carrying tales?"

"Reasonably so," he told her, "but we'll run a check on him. About Thursday, feed this item to Graney with the progress report."

She took the paper, reading aloud: "At Station 6200 plus 12 a small vein of silver ore was encountered. This stringer is not commercial but does indicate penetration into the metalliferous area. We can expect to meet faulted strata at any time now." She put the paper on her desk. "You didn't hit silver, did you?"

"Not a smidgin of it," he said. "Also, we're well past 6200. But if Graney passes this word along, it won't take much time until Jason gets an echo of it. Then we'll be sure Graney is a traitor."

"I'll make you a bet, Mike. Even if Lock is caught in the act, Jason, the old softy, won't fire him."

"I hope not," Kendall said. "We want him for a pipe line into van Zandt's organization. We'll find a use for him."

A week later, on his morning session with Jason Tarow on the telephone, he asked the promoter, "Anything new, Jason?"

"Nothing on this end, Mike. By the way, have you hit any more silver leads in the tunnel?"

"Just that one insignificant stringer. I'm not sure I could even find it now. Why, you want to develop it?"

Tarow laughed. "Not me. But one of our leading mining tycoons was inquiring. I told him it was nothing."

"Wonder how he heard about it? I suppose one of our men was in town, passed it off as a big strike. It doesn't matter, I guess."

"It's a good thing to know, though," Tarow said pointedly. "But Mike, more important, I've been expecting every day that you would work out of this production slump. But you don't. When can I expect good footage reports again?"

Graney must be bending an ear, Kendall thought. He went into a long song and dance about machinery breakdowns, weather, sick mules, and manpower trouble. Before he was through he could almost hear Tarow sobbing over the long line.

When he hung up the receiver, Fran Diamond shook her head. "You don't mind laying it on thick, do you?" she asked. "Think Lock fell for that too?"

"We've got him primed for anything," he said. "And when the time comes, we'll exploit him to the limit." He reached for his fur cap. "Keep 'er running, kid. I'm going over to the tunnel."

The path down the shoulder of the coulee was cut waist-deep in snow. In the crisp bright air, Kendall strode along, full of the vigor of well-being. He was thinking of the dread he had brought to this job. He had lain awake nights going through failure a hundred ways—the disaster of fire or explosion or premature break-through. As he had gotten the job strung out, as things fell smoothly into place, the fears receded. The rock formation continued to hold up, with only moderate seepage and little need for timbering.

He shook his head. It was too good to be true. In view of the type of formation the drift must penetrate, they ought soon to be fighting both bad ground and heavy seepage. He caught himself wondering if, when they met trouble, the old fear would come back, the blind panic. He hoped not. But deep in the back of his mind something stirred. He shivered, deliberately thrusting it aside. Time enough, he told himself, time enough.

He heard the clatter of iron wheels over rail joints and hurried down to the canyon bed. Missouri raised his willow withe as the white mule plodded past toward the tunnel. Kendall swung up into the last empty of the string and rode on into the damp warm air of the tunnel.

Christmas being on a Friday, Kendall had ordered a carryall on runners to come to Blue Grouse on Thursday afternoon. A half chinook was blowing, the air was mild, and melting snow ran in little rivulets down bank and slope. The long vehicle pulled up between the bunk-houses and men ran to get aboard. Those who had decided to stay in camp watched with something of envy.

When the sled was loaded, Kendall waved his hand for silence.

"Have a good time, boys, but don't overdo it," he said. "We need you here at Blue Grouse, you're all damned good men—a cheer went up "—good men, and I can't spare you. So for every man who reports for his regular shift Monday, Miss Diamond has a Christmas bonus—full pay for the skipped shifts between now and then!" A real yell went up this time. "One last thing, then you can have your celebration—there are people in Juniper who don't like you and me and Blue Grouse. Now you know we're past Station 6600." The few who knew how far past kept silent. "So when certain parties try to pump you, as they will, just drink their free liquor and tell 'em '6600 feet in' and let it go at that. That will rattle their slats for 'em."

"That we'll do, Mike!" "Hooraw fur Blue Grouse!" "We'll have a drink for you. lads!"

The driver popped his whip above the ears of his team, and the noisy crowd was off in a splashing shower of melting snow.

Kendall turned to the men who stayed, some of them looking glum. "I didn't tell you, boys, but we're shut down here until Monday, though your pay goes on. Just keep the fires going and the pipes from freezing. We've got a big dinner coming up tomorrow, the best of everything Juniper could provide. And a big entertainment tomorrow night."

The dinner was a huge success on Christmas Day. Afterward Kendall contributed a couple of demijohns of whisky to arouse the men from their torpor. Irish Murfree sawed away on his fiddle, several of the men danced hornpipes and cakewalks until out of breath. Then Fran Diamond sang the old mining camp songs for them, even the ones with twenty-five verses, until the sentimental mood could have been measured with a yardstick. Kendall enjoyed it as much as anyone, for once taking on more drinks than he needed and not greatly caring.

It was the shank of the evening when the whisky ran out. The party dwindled away. The noisy celebrants staggered off, bellowing, to their respective bunkhouses. Kendall helped Fran Diamond into her coat.

"Thank you for singing, Fran," he said, carefully trying to keep his words from slurring. "You have a fine voice, and the boys enjoyed it. So did I."

They walked down the path in the sheen of the starlight to Fran's cabin.

"How's it happen you din—didn't go to Juniper, kid?" he asked. "Kinda lonesome here, away from everybody."

She paused before her door, her face a pale loveliness in the soft light. "Nothing there for me, Mike," she said gently. "No folks, few friends. I was as well off here. Now, don't you think you had better head for home and bed?"

"See you inside first," he said stubbornly.

She shrugged and opened the door. She fumbled for the cord of the electric light. The room sprang into light as she turned the key. She looked at Kendall, hesitated a moment, and said, "Come in, then."

He stepped inside and closed the door behind him. The room was warm, the air touched faintly by the odor of Fran's perfume and cologne. The liquor fumes rose dizzyingly in him. He leaned for support against the jamb of the door. He watched her as she hung coat and scarf in the wardrobe. She took something from a dresser drawer and came toward him.

"Mike, I want…" she began.

A sudden hunger shook him. Two steps and she was in his arms. He tipped her chin up, seeing her eyes wide with surprise. He kissed her, finding her lips soft and sweet, remembering with odd clarity that this was the second time. He drew her close, feeling the long lissome curves of her slim body against him. For a long moment she seemed to surrender, lips and arms and body, her bosom thrusting at his chest.

Then she turned her head away. With almost absurd ease she twisted out of his arms. She stood looking at him, her back to the end of the bed, breathing faster than normal, her eyes holding sympathy and sadness.

"You shouldn't have done that, Mike," she said.

"I know—'m a damn' fool, Fran. Too many drinks, I guess. May I 'pologize?"

"Not all your fault, Mike. I—I think I wanted you to. I was lonely, too. Maybe more so because of this." She held out her hand. "Jason sent it out with the driver of the carryall."

He shook his head to clear the fog, trying to focus on the stone on her finger, glinting with shards of pure light.

"A diamond, huh? Appropriate. Diamond for Miss Diamond. Congrashulations, Fran. Jason's good man."

"So Mike, I may be Mrs. Jason Tarow after all," she said. "I have the ring. But where is Jason on this Christmas night?"

She flung out her hands in a gesture of anger and despair.

He took a step toward her.

With a sob, she took hold of his arm and turned him toward the door. Before he knew what happened, he found himself outside in the gleaming night.

Fran Diamond stood in the shaft of light from the open door. He thought he caught the glint of tears in her eyes.

"Go home, Mike, before we both forget that I am now an engaged woman—engaged *in absentia*. Merry Christmas."

He felt the softness of her kiss on his cheek. Then the door closed and he was alone in the starlight. He stumbled down the path, feeling very sorry for himself, annoyed at Fran for turning him out so rudely. There were other girls, he thought, wiping a maudlin tear from his eye. Pretty Ruth, for instance—would she turn him away on a snowy Christmas night? And then he had to grin sourly at himself, knowing she would.

At his cabin he struggled out of his clothes and piled into bed. On the verge of sleep a clear ray of logic pierced his stupor. Why all this self-pity? He was foot-loose and fancy-free, and hadn't any intention of being anything else. Why worry about the boss's fiancée and the millionaire's daughter? But damn it, they were pretty girls, both of them. If he ever did settle down...

The thaw congealed right after Christmas and the weather turned bitter. For a few days after the episode at the cabin there was a little constraint between him and Fran, but it soon wore off and the work went on, work that absorbed the energies and the hours of all of them, leaving little time for insight or recrimination.

There was another thaw in January. Then a swirling blizzard made the surface so hazardous that Kendall had his crew rig life lines from camp to tunnel. In mid-February a particularly vicious storm brought a complete shutdown for two days. After that he put the men back to work in spite of the cold—if he hadn't, an epidemic of cabin fever would have led to bloodshed. The interminable card and checker games were already bringing old friendships to a surly end. Work was the cure, and Kendall kept them at it.

Spring is not a sudden thing in the high altitudes of Montana: a gradual lengthening of days, so it was light now at breakfast and suppertime; a little warmth in the sunlight, the sun brighter and higher in the sky. Kendall noted that the creek began to talk to itself under the ice. At night the bunkhouse fires were banked more lightly, and the snow cover was settling.

On a day in mid-March, Kendall came out of the tunnel with a new worry to plague him. Not that it hadn't been expected, but the sight of the bad ground had sent a feather of fear along his spine. He and Tom Hughes had brought in Irish Murfree's crew with caps and stulls, and started placing sets every six feet. And with the faulted rock came the spurt of water, soaking the men and the machines, swelling the inky runnel along the mine track.

Kendall realized he had been living in a fool's paradise, thinking he had laid the ghost of the Lobchick. Now he felt the familiar flutter in his stomach, the cloying dryness of fear in the roof of his mouth. He shook his head and started up the slope toward camp, under a sky gray with the threat of snow.

A tram clanked toward him on the narrow-gauge, the white mule plodding its patient way. But young Bentz was driving. Seeing that, Kendall held up a hand for the kid to stop.

"Where's Missouri?" he asked.

"Down sick with a misery," Bentz told him. "Tom Hughes asked me to take over Sweetheart for a day or two."

"Did he say what ailed the old rebel?"

"Terrible gut-ache of some kind. Real sick, Tom said."

Kendall dismissed him with a gesture. Bentz grinned, flipped the reins, and moved off toward the tunnel entrance.

Kendall turned toward the bunkhouses. He didn't like having a man sick. He had been lucky so far. On the job he had insisted on the men working safely, and by that or by sheer luck he had had only minor accidents, a man with three fingers clipped off under a snubbed line, another with a broken leg from a fall on the ice. Beyond that, he had shipped two tunnel men into Juniper with miner's pneumonia, one of whom was already back on the job. As he walked into the warmth of the bunkhouse, he crossed his fingers.

The air was gamy inside, rich with the stink of wet wool, tobacco, sweat, and burnt wood. He saw a man in a bunk at the far side of the room and walked over. The lank form of the Missourian was doubled up in the bunk, the blankets twisted.

"Feeling bad, Missou'?" Kendall asked.

The skinner turned his gaunt flushed face. "Got me a misery, boss. It's plum wrenchin' my gut out. Never had nothin' hurt so bad in my borned days. Even whisky won't touch 'er."

Kendall put a hand on the man's forehead, finding it flaming with fever.

"We're going to get you help, Missou', right away. You take it as easy as you can."

As he hurried to the office the first big wet snowflakes were drifting down, as soft and smothering as gray goose feathers.

CHAPTER TWELVE

He pushed the office door shut and strode to the telephone. He spun the crank hard. Receiver to ear, he said over his shoulder, "Fran, get out the medicine chest. We've got a sick man."

Jason Tarow answered.

Kendall said, "Jason, we've got a man down and it looks serious. Will you get Doc Von Bulow to the telephone as fast as you can?"

"Certainly, Mike. Not more than a few minutes," Tarow said, and hung up. Kendall blessed him for his quick understanding.

"What do you find, Fran?" he asked, walking over to the desk.

"Opium pills, paregoric, laudanum. I'll take some of it over and try to ease him," she said, gathering vials and bottles.

"Good girl. I'll wait for the call."

She was back by the time the telephone rang.

"Dot sounds like a nize case of inflammation of de vermiform appendix," the doctor told Kendall, his voice thin over the hum of the line. "Dot man needs surgery pooty soon, or he's a deader. Mike, you got to bring him to me over the mountain some way."

"I hate to try it, the shape he's in, Doc," Kendall said. "And it's coming on snow. Can't you come to Blue Grouse?"

"Not even a schlim chance, Mike. Two confinement cases, vun already in labor. Annuder due any time, she scares me bad, the conformation, you understand, it is not right. I do not dare to leave Juniper. You must get your man here somehow."

"If we must, then. Fran is here. Give her instructions on what to do to help him stand the trip."

She took the receiver. "Yes, Doctor. Wrap him warmly—ice packs on the abdomen, yes—laudanum, yes, I've given him that. All right, Doctor. We'll do our best."

Kendall wasn't wasting time. The weather looked bad, with the snow falling heavily now. He picked a crew of tough, wiry men with youth on their side—Bentz, Eddie Lamb, Irish Murfree, and Tod Skiffen. They hitched the best team in camp to the light bobsled. They filled the bed of it with hay, piled it high with blankets and robes, and flung a tarp over it. They carried the Missourian from the bunkhouse and laid him in the sled. Heavily doped as he was, he still groaned a little with pain. Fran Diamond climbed in beside him, pulling a blanket up around her.

The first steep stretch was bad enough. But as they hit the switchbacks toward the slope of the ridge, Kendall saw that the storm had hit here earlier than in the canyon. Drifts were deepening at every windbreak, and the wind itself grew harder. Bentz, who was driving, called for shovels.

"Old Man Winter still can give a few licks," Tod Skiffen said, panting.

"And dom good ones at that," Irish Murfree agreed, wiping the rime from his long mustache. "All right, Benny, give her a try."

Kendall and the others stood aside as Bentz flicked his reluctant team with the whiplash. As the sled pulled forward, Kendall saw that Fran Diamond, seated beside the prostrate Missouri, was blue with cold.

"Take her place for a while, Eddie," he said to the Lamb boy. "She's got to get her circulation going by walking."

The dumb boy nodded. He climbed into the sled and helped Fran to rise. Kendall helped her over the sideboards, caught her as she staggered.

"Oh, Mike," she moaned, "my feet feel like old sticks."

"That's why you have to walk," he told her, putting an arm around her shoulders. "Come on, now, left, right...."

By the time they reached the next bend, she was panting. But the pink was back in her cheeks, and feeling had returned to her feet. "That's better," she said. "I was half frozen and didn't know it."

"You'll make it now. How was Missouri?"

"Sleeping soundly. He ought to, he has enough laudanum in him to knock out John L. Sullivan. The ice pack must help, too, for he isn't as restless."

"Maybe he's frozen solid. You'd better get back in the the wagon too. This storm is getting worse, I'm afraid."

"I'll make it to the top of the hill," she said. "Give Eddie a breather."

A March blizzard in Montana is a fearsome thing. As if the last of the winter devils is driving down the wind, the blizzard howls flat across the land, biting through the warmest of clothing, hiding every road and path and landmark in a swirling nothingness of gray-white. The full fury of it met them when they came out at the top of the ridge.

Kendall opened his mouth to shout and the force of the wind sucked the breath from his lungs. The team, plastered into snowy ghosts, stopped as if they had run into a wall. Bentz urged them forward, finally resorting to the hard lash to make them move.

Turning, Kendall picked up Fran and bundled her into the sled. He and Eddie Lamb pulled blankets and tarp clear over her, and in a few breaths the wagon box on the sled was a mounded heap of snow.

Kendall, with Eddie Lamb beside him, lowered his head and walked in front of the sled. Just one break, he thought, this road is carved out of the rock and through the trees. We can't possibly lose it. But even as the thought ran through his mind, he felt Eddie Lamb's hand on his arm. The boy pulled him aside, shaking his head.

"But that's the road," Kendall said, dull with cold.

Eddie Lamb motioned Kendall to stay put. With his long-handled shovel he probed the white drift beyond their feet. Sudden and soundless, the snow dropped away, exposing a gaping pit. The boy tottered at the edge of it. Kendall yanked him back from the forty-foot drop into the rocks.

With his free arm he hugged the boy. "Thanks, kid," he yelled above the whine of the wind. "You lead the way, then. I'll pass on your signals to Bennie."

The boy moved ahead confidently, face turned to the driving wind. This, Kendall knew, was Eddie's back yard, he must know every foot of the terrain. Besides, he owned the clear perception of youth and the bravery of the familiar. Kendall followed him, careful to walk in his very footsteps. Peering through the murk, he passed Eddie's signals along to the muffled statue of white on the bobsled that was Bennie Bentz. They moved on, foot by tortured foot, horses and men hardly able to endure it.

Then they were off the bare ridge and into the shelter of the trees. The surcease was merciful. Out of the slash of the wind, the air seemed almost warm. They hit drifts up to the bellies of the horses, and they shoveled. They freed the sled and shoveled again. They were all sick with weariness, but it was plain exertion now. The intimate threat of death that had faced them on the ridgetop had faded. Kendall knew that making Juniper now was only a matter of time.

And it was. In the early evening Bentz halted the sled in front of the frame building that was Dr. Von Bulow's hospital. The weary, frostbitten men clambered stiffly out. They pulled the tarpaulin, its coating of ice crackling, from Missouri and the girl. Kendall helped Fran to the ground.

The little doctor and two orderlies came hurrying out.

"You made it, Mike. How iss your man?"

"Fran says a little better. Not moaning so much."

"Maybe not a good sign. But anyvays he iss alive," the doctor said. "Handle him easy, boys. Ve get his clothes off, get him to bed."

As the orderlies moved into the building with the stretcher carrying Missouri, Fran said, "And your other patients, Doctor?"

"Vun of dem, a seven-pound baby boy, the mother fine. The other—I joost can't talk, Miss Diamond. An hour ago, I lose both of them. A sad, sad thing."

"Oh, the poor things!" Fran exclaimed. "And hard on you, Doctor."

He did not answer. Then he shook himself, as if to force the memory aside. He looked at them. "You peoples, maybe a touch of frostbite, no? You want to come in, I look you over?"

"Better not, Doc," Kendall said. "We'll make it to the hotel and some hot food. That will fix us. I'll be over later to check on Missouri. If we went in there now, we'd thaw out too fast."

It was two hours later when Kendall leaned back in his chair, sipping his third cup of strong coffee. He had soaked in a hot bath, downed two steaming toddies, and dressed as presentably as he could. In the dining room of the Elkhorn he found the other five and Jason Tarow.

"By George, Mike, I'm proud of you!" the little man said, pumping Kendall's hand. "All of you are included. A bold brave thing, that trip, and I know you saved the man's life. I've ordered the finest dinner, the best steaks, that the Elkhorn can provide. Let's sit down now, I know you are all famished. Fran, my dear, you sit next to me."

The dinner was superb, expertly served, and of course garnished with the sauce of hunger. Kendall, glancing around the table, smiled at this motley group so misplaced in the genteel atmosphere of the dining room, with its crystal and silver and deep carpets. All of them, except Jason Tarow, were in their rough, heavy winter clothes. He was his usual dapper self, in high wing collar and black broadcloth suit. Bentz had one hand bandaged, Tod Skiffen's right ear was red and swollen, and Murfree claimed he had frostbitten a couple of toes. But none of them were overawed by their surroundings, not even Eddie Lamb, who certainly had never been in such luxurious surroundings before.

Tarow clicked open the case of his watch and checked the time. With an exclamation, he stood up.

"Fran, Mike, I hate to do this. But I have just minutes to make the night train. Long Sam Carlson is getting better, and has been yelling his head off that he wants to see me. I told him I'd see him in the morning, so I've got to get to Helena on the midnight. Will you all forgive me? I hate it like sin. But you know Long Sam."

Kendall saw the disappointment brush Fran's lovely face. But she did not protest. Tarow patted her on the shoulder, shook hands anew around the table, and was gone.

When dinner was over, Kendall signed the check for Tarow and stood up.

"I don't think Doc will operate on Missouri tonight, but the old guy might be scared in his strange surroundings," Kendall said. "I think I'll go over to see him. Anyone want to go along?"

"Why, I'll go," Fran said, her eyes meeting Kendall's glance. Nothing better to do—now. Eddie Lamb pointed vigorously at himself. The others begged off.

In the lobby Kendall said, "Wait a minute, I want to make a call." At the telephone in the hall he had the operator ring the Hagen residence. The maid answered.

"No, they ain't here. The Missus and the Mister, they went to Helena two days ago. Missus is ailing again. Miss Ruth? Why, she went to Helena too. They're all taking the baths at Broadwater. They won't be back until next week."

Kendall hung up, with a let-down feeling. Lucky Jason, he thought. Then he slowed in midstride. Was this more than coincidence? For Fran's peace of mind, he decided to say nothing. He took her arm as they walked down the steps into the blustering wind.

The snow had ceased, and the walk the few blocks to the hospital was not unpleasant. When they got there, the doctor was not there, and Missouri was asleep under opiates so they couldn't see him. They made their way back toward the hotel.

At the main street intersection, deserted now as the other streets in the raw cold, Kendall saw two men approaching under the blue glare of the arc light. One of them was Phil van Zandt. And as Eddie stiffened and clutched at Kendall's arm, Kendall knew that the lean hulk of a man with him. the man with the twisted black beard and eyes that glowed red in the street light, must be Claude Lamb.

Van Zandt stopped at the curb. But Claude Lamb strode forward. He pointed a bony finger at the boy.

"They said ye were back, ye ungrateful limb o' Satan! How sharper than a serpent's tooth is a thankless child!" he cried.

"He's no child of yours, Claude Lamb," Fran Diamond said spiritedly.

"Not mine? I raised him from a pup. I fed him and clothed him, when his father, my own brother, wasted his substance on whisky and women. I taught him the ways of the bird on the wing and the fish in the water, and the path of the roe deer in the wilderness."

Kendall put his arm around the boy's shoulder. He could feel Eddie shaking pitifully. Claude Lamb's tirade went on.

"There ain't no gratitude. I warned his father time and again not to disturb the secrets of Castle Mountain, searching for the devil's gold. He did not listen. Where is he now? Drowned and lost forever in the dank depths. My own brother, punished for his greed. And you, Eddie Lamb! I warned you not to go under the mountain. But you and your wild ways—you hire out to this rascal, and you dig and delve in the virgin rock. Your punishment is at hand. It is my duty to see to it. A lesson to learn, Eddie Lamb. Prepare yourself."

"Leave this boy alone," Kendall said. "Van Zandt, if this is one of your dogs, call him off."

"What he does, he does for himself," van Zandt said piously. But he was smiling thinly.

"I'm not in the mood for foolishness," Kendall said. "Lamb, get out of the way." He moved forward.

Claude Lamb flung out a long arm, grabbed a handful of Kendall's coat, and spun him aside. Kendall was not prepared for the man's amazing strength. He staggered, slipped from the curb and went down in the slippery snow. He was struggling to his feet when Fran screamed.

"Hold it, Kendall," van Zandt said softly. He had his hand thrust into the pocket of his coat. He may not have a gun, Kendall thought. But if he has, he's tough enough to use it. He's got me coppered.

So Kendall stood helpless, watching Claude Lamb pull a braided quirt from under his long coat. Before Eddie could run, his uncle slashed him across face and shoulders viciously, once, twice. The boy sank to his knees in the snow, trying to cover his face from the slashing leather.

Fran Diamond darted forward. She snatched at the quirt. Claude Lamb stepped aside, palmed the butt of the quirt and laid it alongside the girl's head. She dropped as if poleaxed, without a sound.

Eddie Lamb went crazy. He leaped full into the circle of the lash, trying to get at his uncle. But he was no match for the older man, who struck again and again, grinning with perverted pleasure.

"Give it to him, Claude!" van Zandt called out. His eyes were shining. There was white spittle at the corners of his lips. He had forgotten Kendall. Kendall dove at him.

The gun fired through the pocket as van Zandt went down. Across the street, glass tinkled. Kendall gave the mineowner a hip throw that sent him pinwheeling along the cobblestones. He tried for him again, but slipped in the snow. He saw van Zandt reaching for his pocket, trying to get the gun from the scorched cloth. Kendall didn't wait. He leaped high in the air, coming down with the heels of his miner's boots square on the man's arm. Van Zandt screamed, screamed again, and fainted.

Kendall came up, twisting toward the sidewalk. Fran was still down. Eddie was on his knees, arms around his head. Now Claude Lamb went up on his toes, bringing the lash screaming across his nephew's shoulders. Eddie sagged. And a figure came from nowhere, to bring with a full sweep of his arm a blued gunbarrel against Claude Lamb's head. There was a thud like a chopped melon. Claude Lamb collapsed, boneless, face down into the snow.

Pete Trump holstered his revolver. He lifted Eddie Lamb to his feet. "What in hell goes on?" he asked.

Kendall picked Fran Diamond up in his arms. The girl moaned softly.

"Van Zandt held a gun on us while Claude Lamb went berserk with that blacksnake," he explained. "You handle it, Pete. I've got to get help for this kid." He started for the Elkhorn.

Fran Diamond's eyes flicked open under long lashes. Dazed for a moment, then they cleared. She gasped, her hand going to her head.

"Are you all right, Fran?" he asked anxiously.

"My head aches," she said, shaking it. "But I'll make it. Put me down, Mike. We must look after Eddie."

He set her on her feet. She clung to him a second, then she went over to Eddie Lamb. She took her handkerchief and dabbed at the oozing welts on both sides of his face.

"The doctor must look at these, Eddie," she said.

The boy nodded, looking at her with the patient adoring eyes of a hurt spaniel. With an effort he made himself tall and straight. Together they started slowly along the street.

"Get Marshal McGown," Trump ordered one of the group of spectators who had gathered. The man hurried away. Trump leaned over van Zandt. "What did you do to this man, Mike? His arm is busted in three places."

"He took a shot at me," Kendall said. "He had more than a broken arm coming. He was fronting for this gorilla."

"Well, give me a hand," Trump said. "We've got to get him to the hospital."

Fran Diamond and Eddie Lamb passed under the full light of the street light. Kendall could see, across her face, the great livid wale of the bruise from the whipstock.

"Help him, hell! He can lie there and rot, for all of me!" he said, and strode after the other two.

CHAPTER THIRTEEN

Irish Murfree came into the office diffidently with hat in hand like an erring schoolboy. Fran's typewriter stopped clicking, and Kendall saw her smile at the Irishman. After three days her bruised face was still angry at the edge of the dressing, and the tip of her nose, frost burned, gleamed with ointment.

"Mavourneen, I see the marks of the beast fade a little day by day," Murfree said.

"I hope so, Irish," she said. "Poor Eddie is the one who looks like he'd been caught in a meat grinder."

"That Claude is the crazy one, all right, like a mad dog. Nor is van Zandt much better, Mike, have ye the time to talk a bit?"

"Irish, you know better than to ask. If it's palaver you want, go ahead."

"Palaver it is indeed, and I'd sooner be shot than bring these words to you, Mike Kendall, but me conscience is killin' me."

"Out with it, man," Kendall said.

"Mike. I think I sold out the job. For less than a mess of pottage even, mind ye. That night of our trip to Juniper with Missouri, and how we made it I'll never know, though thank the good God we were in time and he's gettin' better from that little pizen snake that were gnawin' at his insides, well that night— Mike, I'm so ashamed of meself..."

Kendall growled, "Irish, be done with the meandering and the blandandering, before I bounce a spittoon off your thick head."

"I will that, Mike. Well, ye see, the cold was in me bones, even after that great steak. So after I left you I had a hot one at the

Miners' Rest, and one at Largo's, and maybe four or foive or some such at Malcom Marshall's place, and a grand spot that is for the weary traveler. But would ye believe it, those three or four thimblefuls av the best, and I was suddenly with drink taken? The sense went out of me head, along with the cold from me bones. I mind I met that little four-eyes works for Tarow, Graney his name is. I greeted him like a long-lost brother and bought him a drink. Then he signals to Malcolm and buys me three, maybe four rounds av the brute. 'Twas then I spilled the beans."

"To Lock Graney? What did you tell him?"

"With his long face, he says the job is going tough. Me, feelin' joy for all the world, laughs in his wizen face and tells him he is insultin' the best hard-rock crew in the West. A foine crew it is, he says, that makes only three thousand fate of hole in four months. So how far are we into the mountain, I says? And he replies, the bold blaggard, eighty-seven hundred plus nineteen fate that very blessed morning."

Kendall braced himself. "So you opened your big mouth?"

"Aye, and put me big foot in it, too. I says, 'Then me old eyes is failing me, for me last shift I made a set under a piece of bad ground, with the front stulls square on Station 102 plus nought nought. Which in minin' parlance,' I says, 'means the workin' face at Blue Grouse is 10,200 feet from the adit. For which pure quill ye can, little man, buy me another round of the same.' He says quick-like, 'That I'll do,' and flips a shiny double eagle to Malcom Marshall. 'Pour until that is gone,' he says, and takes out the door like the Black Bitch of Ballyknock was right at his coattails. I had me a couple more from the bottle, and then the whisky turned to lead in me stomach, as I begun to feel the meanin' of what I had done. I didn't like the way yon Graney had snapped up me words. So I says to Marshall, 'Let me have me change,' and with that I winds up the staircase to me bed. And since that moment, I have been seeking the courage to confess me sin."

"Irish, may that teach you to leave the poteen alone," Kendall admonished. "But I doubt if there is great harm done. Van Zandt would have learned one of these days his reports were faked."

"Van Zandt!" Murfree exclaimed. "Graney is his spy?"

"Right. And we've been using him to keep van Zandt quiet."

"So Murfree had to go and make a bull. Now the Dutchman will be at us hammer and tongs, save the mark."

"Mike slowed him down, though," Fran Diamond said, her fingers going to the dressing on her face. "Jason said van Zandt's arm is broken in three places."

"Too bad it weren't his head," Murfree said, scowling.

"Let's forget that dirty business," Kendall said. "Irish, did you take Tod Skiffen and look over that snowfield?"

"That I did. And I can't say I like the looks of it, boss."

"What's the situation?"

Murfree took the chewed stub of a pencil from his overall pocket. On a piece of foolscap he traced an elongated upright Y. Below the base of the Y he drew two slanting lines, roughly in the shape of an inverted V, the left arm somewhat more toward the horizontal than the right one, which was only some twenty-five degrees from the perpendicular.

"The heavy snow, the winter's snow plus the heavy wet snow of our last storm, lies trapped in this Y, here and here." He pointed with the pencil stub. "Fifty or sixty foot of it in some places, I would judge. It all rests on a spine of rock. Below the spine—" he indicated the inverted V—"this right arm is the natural path for any slide. Yon mountain is scarred and chewed by the marks of them. But this year, with such a mighty burden of snow and ice, this left arm might steer part of the sliding field our way. And the chute of it points like a highwayman's pistol, right at our workings down in the canyon."

"It could do a lot of harm, Irish?"

"Aye, that it could. How many ton of ice and snow and scrap rock and down logs the good God himself only knows. On top of the entrance, and smashing the boilerhouse. 'Twould set us back for months."

"Maybe for good," Kendall said grimly, "if Jason couldn't get additional money to finance the extra costs. What's your guess, Irish, on the chances of us catching a slide down that left groove?"

"With luck, we're safe enough. I did some talking to Eddie Lamb—or rather writin', and it's a dom poor writer I am—about yon slide. Him and his dad and that devil Claude had a prospect on the mountain south of here. They could see the slope of Castle from their cabin door. Of four years, he says the snowslide come down three—twict down the right arm, once down both of 'em. That last there was a big chinook blew for three days before the slide."

Kendall rubbed his jaw. "Any chance to blow it ourselves?"

" 'Twould be dangerous to interfere with the course of nature, I have a hunch," the Irishman said. "Look, boss. Your tellyphone line cuts across the bottom of the slide path on its way to Juniper. Why not fix up a tellyphone on the line, and post young Eddie to kape an eye on the brute? He could ring the bell a certain way to signal 'all well,' or 'run for your life,' if she showed any signs of coming down the left track."

"That's a good idea, Irish. At least we'll be doing something. I'll get together with Tom Hughes and Steve Hradic about clearing the works and the tunnel fast, in case of a warning. Send Eddie over."

They set Eddie up in a tent near the telephone line, with grub and stove, and a telephone boxed and wired on a nearby tree. For the boy it was a picnic. He had his .22 rifle and lots of ammunition. And all he had to do was stay in the vicinity of the rock ridge by his tent, keep watch on the slide, and report morning and evening by ringing the code ring Kendall had given him. After examining the slide menace himself, Kendall felt this watch by the boy gave enough extra precaution so he did not need to shut down the job. They were making good yardage in the tunnel, and he hated to lose even an hour's work.

When you live with a menace long enongh, it fades to the back of your mind, still there, but something to be lived with. So Kendall found the menace of the slide as several days went by. While the midday warmth caused black streams of water to seep from under the massed snowfield, the temperature dropped at night and the melting of the mass was gradual. Barring a strong chinook wind, the danger was gradually decreasing.

So Kendall was in a comfortable state of mind as he came out of the tunnel this day after checking with Hughes on the result of the morning blast. The rock formation was still holding, the shot rounds were breaking clean, and here outside the sun was shining. He started to turn up the steep path toward camp, to report to Jason Tarow. He heard a shout and paused.

"Wait up, Mike Kendall!" Perley Fahnestock yelled. The prospector came hurrying, panting a little. He stopped, took off his battered hat, and mopped his brow with a blue bandanna.

"There's hell to pay and no pitch hot, Mike," he said.

"Somebody picking on you, old-timer?"

"No, dammit! It's you that's under the gun. Claude Lamb, that fleabit, addled lunatic, is going to bring the mountain down on your tunnel!" He sat down on a balk of timber. "Whew! Fastest time anybody ever made down the Blue Grouse canyon, I bet you."

Kendall sat down beside him. "Let's have it, Perley. You've seen Lamb?"

"Seen him? He stayed at my cabin all night, never takin' his hand off'n his rifle. And he stood over me s'morning and made me cook his breakfast, all the time rantin' on like a crazy man. Too damn' bad I didn't have no wolf poison, he'da got it. Tied me up, too, when he left. But he don't know fur shucks about knots. Five minutes and I was outen the rope, and hightailin' it here."

"What's the man up to?"

"A sound enough idee, for a crazy man. He showed me his pack, give me a peek inside. Mike, he's got damn' near a case of dynamite in it. He ever falls down, they won't find a big enough piece to bury. What he's up to, he bragged to me, he's going to blow that snowfield yander down on top of the tunnel."

"He knew about it from the old Lamb prospect, I guess. But why, Perley? What possible motive can he have?"

The prospector shook his head, his gray beard wagging emphatically. "You sort it out of his crazy talk, I cain't. Something about violatin' the virgin rock, and the lust for gold and the sin thereof—maybe you never heard the way Claude garbles Holy Writ—and some more about his dead brother and the punishment of the water and the rock. On and on, but still he has this sly gleam in his eye. Once during the night I seen him pawing over a stack of gold coin, when he thought I was asleep. Damn' little sleep I got with that maniac and his rifle and his giant powder under my roof. But crazy or not, he means business, Mike. If I was you, I'd take steps. And damn' sudden."

Kendall stood up. He put a hand on the old man's shoulder.

"Thanks, Perley. The boys and I will never forget this. Now beat it up to camp and get a bait of grub. I'm appointing you to take care of Miss Diamond, and see that she keeps out of danger."

Perley Fahnestock chuckled. "Kinda ancient for a purty little gal like that, but I might surprise myself. See you later, Mike."

Kendall's mind had been racing in a fast appraisal of the situation. There were obvious steps, to clear the tunnel and get everyone out of the danger area, and to stop Claude Lamb. The first was easy. He ran to the boilerhouse.

"Kill the air," he called to Tod Skiffen. "Bleed the tank."

As he raced out to the switchbox outside, he heard the compressor clank to a stop as Skiffen shut down the steam engine. Above the hissing of exhaust steam, he pulled the switch open, closed it again. Three times, three times again, and a long five seconds open. He thrust it closed again and left it there.

He did not wait to see if the signals were acted upon. His men had the word, and they were not fools. He turned and ran toward camp. As he passed the stables he yelled at the hostler to saddle the horse and bring it to the office, and fast.

He burst into the office and wrenched open the tall cupboard. Fran Diamond stared at him, her eyes wide with surprise.

He checked the .30-30 Winchester, and thumbed shells into the loading gate. He dumped extra cartridges into his pocket and slid the strap of his field glasses around his neck. Rifle at the trail, he stopped a moment.

"Fran, that crazy Claude Lamb is going to try to blow that avalanche down on us. I've washed out the work, the men will be out of the tunnel in a little while. Keep them here, out of either slide area, until the thing is decided one way or another."

"But where are you going?" she cried.

"Up to Eddie Lamb's post. I've got to stop that maniac some way. Watch the mountain, you'll know if I succeeded," he said, with a touch of grim humor. He opened the door and was gone.

As the horse galloped through the slop and wet of the supply road, Kendall considered his plan. He shook his head—a long shot, but the only feasible way to intercept Claude Lamb. If Kendall was wrong, if the left face was not too steep and broken for a man to cross, then Blue Grouse was doomed. If, as he figured, Claude Lamb must come up over the mountain above Perley Fahnestock's prospect hole and swing around the shoulder from the right, then there was a chance. And thanks to the old man's ready warning, Kendall could well reach the slide area ahead of Lamb. At least, he thought, no matter what happens to the job, nobody will get killed now. Except perhaps Lamb—or me.

At the top of the long slope he turned the horse off the road into the brush and broken rock. The slope steepened. He dismounted and tied the horse. He took rifle and glasses and scrambled up through buckbrush and aspen and shattered rock, found the telephone line, moved along it to Eddie Lamb's tent.

Eddie Lamb was standing by the little sheet-iron stove, a frying pan in one hand, a half-eaten rabbit leg in the other. His mouth opened as he saw Kendall. His glance flicked to the rifle.

"Your uncle Claude, Eddie," Kendall explained swiftly. "He's up there on the mountain somewhere with a knapsack full of dynamite. He plans to blow the snowfield down on the tunnel. It's up to us to stop him."

The boy's face went pale, the marks of his uncle's lash showing as livid streaks against the pallor. But he did not hesitate. He got the .22 from the tent, and the small telescope Kendall had given him to watch the slide area. He hitched up his pants, grinned at Kendall, and jerked a thumb toward the cliff.

"Just a minute," Kendall told him. He went to the telephone box and spun the crank. Fran Diamond answered, her voice breathless.

"I'm at Eddie's camp, Fran," he told her. "I'll call when we have news. Don't let anyone follow me. If the two of us can't handle this, twenty would do worse. So long, now."

"Mike, take care of yourself," she pleaded. "Don't take ..."

Gently he hung up the receiver. He picked up his rifle.

"Come on, Eddie. Let's go," he said.

CHAPTER FOURTEEN

They moved up through the broken rock, up the spine of the ridge, the avalanche basin dropping off to the right, the cliff above Blue Grouse off beyond a narrowing swale to the left. The rocks were bare, and the snow patches in the hollows were melting, but a chill wind searched their bones and made Kendall turn the collar of his short Mackinaw up around his face.

Eddie Lamb, lithe as a cat, led the way up the narrowing spine. Finally they came out on a flattened outcrop, the slope dropping away in loose detritus on each side. Two hundred yards above lay the lower edge of the snowfield, its foot supported by the jutting overhang of the mountain shoulder. As it slanted upward to the right, the immense mass of snow and ice was held in a shallow cup. From under its lower edge black streams of water honeycombed the mass and dribbled away in the slide rock below.

Panting, they dropped prone against the rock, the swell of it giving them a slight but welcome protection from the cutting edge of the wind. Kendall took his field glasses from the case. Propped on his elbows, he scanned the snowfield and the mountain slope beyond. Nothing moved. Turning, he swept the glasses over the left-hand slope, covering as much of its abrupt face as he could see. He was about to give up, when with an exclamation, he swung them back to cover a faint movement. Then he grinned—clear in the lenses he saw a buck deer at the edge of the stunted timber. Claude Lamb had not come that way, then. He would come from the right if he came at all.

They watched for some time, Kendall with the field glasses, Eddie Lamb with the little telescope. After a while, the rocks blurred and danced and a man had to look away. The spring sun was warm on the back, in the woods behind them a bird made a racketing cry. Kendall hitched himself into a more comfortable position.

Suddenly Eddie Lamb tapped him on the shoulder, pointing. Kendall jerked the glasses up. At the right edge of the snowfield, where it merged into bare rock and the twisted brown-green of juniper, a figure appeared. Claude Lamb, bearded and sinister, his body bowed forward by the weight of the knapsack. He did not hesitate at the rim of the snow. He plunged out across the slope, splashing through the runoff water, ignoring the ponderous mass poised on the mountainside.

Kendall shook his head. He unslung his rifle and jacked a shell into the chamber. Aiming ahead of Lamb, he dropped the bead into the notch of the rear sight and squeezed the trigger. The bullet splashed mud and water just ahead of the man. The noise of the shot racketed back and forth from hill to cliff. Claude Lamb stood motionless a second and then dove for cover.

Kendall stood up, waving. "Lamb! That was a warning. Go back. Try to keep on and I'll shoot to kill."

His answer came quickly. From behind Lamb's boulder, the slam of a shot, a drift of black powder smoke. A silver splash of lead sprang out on the rock by Kendall's foot. Rock chips stung his legs. He dropped down into shelter in a hurry.

"Eddie," he said, "That uncle of yours is plumb loco."

The boy nodded, his face drawn and harsh. His fingers went up to touch the welts still prominent on his cheek. He hitched himself forward, cradling the .22 in his arms.

There was a shout. The cupped side of the mountain made a sounding board for Claude Lamb's great preaching voice.

"In the Lord Jehovah's name will I smite thee hip and thigh! You wicked will cease from troubling and go weary to your rest."

Cran-n-g! A bullet whined off the rock and the two men ducked. "Nephew, deceit becomes you like the tongue of an adder, wickedness is sweet in your mouth. I will lead you to the rock that is higher than I, I will drown you in the noise of many waters. Eddie Lamb, like your father before you, I will dig for you a pit, and you shall fall therein!"

Kendall glanced at the boy, saw that his face was sick with disgust.

"You are descended from the loins of Lucifer, Eddie Lamb," Claude bellowed. "I needed gold, gold to convert the heathen, the free gold of the Winkin Jack. I still need it. Nor will man stand in the way of the Lord, hallelujah! Once before I unleashed the thunderbolt of the Lord, and the Philistines were cleansed by the great waters."

Kendall flung a quick shot at the sound of the voice. For a moment a great silence followed the slam of the shot. Then Claude Lamb began again.

"You, Kendall, yours is the abomination of desolation. Ye seek to delve into the secrets of God's mountain. Today that will end, you and all your works will die under the thunderbolt of the Lord, and me, His humble instrument. Kendall, you hound of hell…"

Before Kendall could stop him, Eddie Lamb was up over the swell of the rock barrier. Beyond, on the edge of the scree, he dropped to one knee and raised the little .22. A bullet spun rock chips from beside him and keened off into empty space. Another snapped viciously overhead. Kendall was up, now, without regard to his own safety, trying to find a target for his rifle.

Eddie Lamb had a mark. The little rifle cracked once, twice, three times, as the boy got off his shots as steady as a metronome. Then, at the edge of the snows, the mountain went up in smoke and flame. The shock of it came up through the rock, a stiff jar at the solar plexus. Rock and snow geysered high, to fall back like a fading fountain. Eddie Lamb had hit his uncle's deadly pack.

Kendall lay motionless and breathless, watching the snow-field. The snow dropped away below the point of the explosion. From above, it began to flow like sand, the surface rippling and crinkling as the thousands of tons got into motion. A tongue of white licked down the slope, and where Claude Lamb had been there was nothing.

Here on the spine of the ridge they were safe enough from what followed. But the awesome shuddering power of it made Kendall's throat go dry, and his heart pound with fear. From both arms of the Y the mass broke up and poured into the old avalanche basin, carrying everything before it, ice and rock and vagrant tree boles. It was an earth-shaking river, a white cloud of snow dust rising high above it. The edge of it lapped up toward their haven. Eddie Lamb buried his head in his arms at the rumble of the rock. Kendall put an arm over the boy's shoulders, watching the slide in fascination and awe.

Then, suddenly, it was over. An absolute silence hung over the valley, as the fog of snow crystals drifted away. Below a great fan of debris, snow and ice with broken trees and torn limbs sticking out of it like raisins in a duff, reached clear into the timber above the road. Surveying it, Kendall swore softly. He could see the telephone poles at each side of the big bowl. But between there was nothing but the white expanse of the slide. The line was gone.

He swept his glasses across the left-hand slope, praying that it was safe. He breathed easier when he saw only one new slide track on the sheer rock, and that a small one. The explosion had evidently relieved the pressure, and channeled the entire snow-field down this right slope. Blue Grouse was safe—from this threat, at least. But in Kendall there grew a strong and unrelenting anger at the man who had triggered this attack, and sent a crazy man to his death—Phil van Zandt.

Eddie Lamb was on his feet now. Kendall saw that the boy's face was still taut and shocked, as if he wanted to cry but couldn't. He patted Eddie on the shoulder.

"Tough going, kid. But you did what you had to, even if the man was your own uncle," he said.

Eddie Lamb nodded slowly. He looked up the slope where Claude Lamb had last stood. Again his hand went up to his face, touching the whip scars. Then his shoulders went back. He looked at Kendall, nodded, and slipping his arm through the strap of the .22, he turned down the ridge toward his tent.

At the campsite Eddie stuffed his clothes into a pack. The two of them made their way down to the main road. Just as they reached the point where Kendall's horse was tied, a buggy came racing toward them. Seeing the two men, Bentz hauled the team to a stop. He wrapped the reins around the whipstock and jumped down, reaching up to help Fran Diamond. Perley Fahnestock, as agile as a goat in spite of the gray whiskers, dropped easily to the road.

"Mike, Mike, are you all right?" Fran Diamond cried, hurrying to him.

"All's well, kid," he said, smiling.

The tenseness washed from her face. She came close to him, putting her forehead against his chest. Her voice muffled, she said, "I—we were so worried, that shooting, and then the blast and the roar of the slide. You might have been—oh, Mike, anything might have happened."

He tipped her chin up, seeing the glint of tears in her eyes.

"But it didn't," he said gently. "We intercepted Lamb, tried to stop him, and in the end a shot blew up the explosive he was carrying. It brought down the slide, but on the proper side of the mountain. It was as simple as that."

"I'll bet it was," she said. "Well, I'll find out from Eddie."

His hand tightened on her arm with a pressure that was almost cruel. "Don't do that, ever, Fran," he said, his voice harsh.

She looked up at him, startled. Then, with her quick intuition, she understood. She nodded.

"Help me into the buggy, Mike," she said, smiling at him.

He boosted her up. Bentz, Perley and Eddie clambered in. Bentz turned the team on the narrow road. Kendall swung up on his horse.

"Any damage to the works?" Kendall asked, before he dropped behind the buggy.

"Tom had all the boys up on the flat, out of harm's way," Bentz told him. "So the one rock that went through the boilerhouse didn't hurt anyone. Busted a steam line, Tod said. He and Irish are already working on it."

"Claude's gone, eh?" Perley Fahnestock asked, his old eyes shrewd.

"For good, Perley. Man carries powder around, liable to have an accident any time," Kendall said.

"Ain't it the truth? Well, in this case, good riddance." The prospector spat downwind and leaned back in the buggy seat, grinning at the world.

Kendall looked at his watch as they came into camp. He was astonished to find that it was less than three hours since he had first been hailed by Perley Fahnestock. The weariness of reaction came over him, and he yawned. An uncharacteristic irritation struck him when he saw all the men standing around, waiting for him. He dismounted and handed the reins of his horse to the hostler.

"Tom, for God's sake, let's knock it off," he said, striding up to his foreman. "It's only midday. Get these men back in the tunnel. We've got hole to make."

Tom Hughes looked at him in surprise, a little resentful. He ordered the men to head back for the job. He himself was the last to go. He looked at Kendall.

Perversely, Kendall maintained his critical attitude. Only at the last moment did the childishness of it strike him.

"Sorry, Tom. Forgive me for being owly. But I saw a man blown to bits a while ago. It's not easy on the nerves."

Hughes looked at him for a long moment, then the frown left his face. "I understand, Mike. Now I'll get the crew back to moving rock."

Fran Diamond closed her ledger with a bang.

"That's that," she said. "But I don't know what good it does with the telephone line out. We might as well be marooned on the moon."

Kendall laughed at her. "Sure strange how anything was ever done before Dr. Bell invented the instrument," he said. "But it will still be a while before Tod Skiffen can do anything about fixing it. You'll have to typewrite your report and send it in on the supply wagon."

"I suppose. But I've felt like a hermit without that line."

"You're getting a touch of cabin fever, kid," he told her. "Too long a winter. Too many men with sweaty shirts and whiskers."

She stretched back, her arms over her head, her blouse taut against the fullness of her bosom.

"Mike, I think you're right. I need to dress up in grand new clothes and a big hat with a sweeping plume. I want Jason to take me to dinner at the Elkhorn, with lights and soft music and tender words. And even more, I need to talk woman-talk with a dozen of the girls, to chatter about children and weddings, and sin and scandal. Is that a sign of cabin fever?"

"It is. Well, when the job is over, you can take all that salary you've piled up and do whatever your heart desires."

"You know what my heart desires," she said, giving him a direct, frank glance. "But that's not my say-so, it's Jason's. As for the other, I'd have to wait a while. All my spare salary has gone into Blue Grouse shares."

"Jason believes in keeping it in the family, then," he said.

"He's a salesman, Mike, as you know. By the way, where is your money going?"

"The same place as yours—back into Blue Grouse."

She laughed, throwing her head back, the long line of her throat smooth above the lace of her collar.

"So Jason Tarow sold us the same bill of goods," she said.

"Yours, I think, is predicated on a different idea," he told her. "But in any case, we'll be rich or broke. So far, our luck has been spectacular. But," he paused, feeling the familiar dryness in his throat, "if we hit water too soon, we may be licked."

"The Blue Grouse crew? Mike, don't be silly."

"I'm scared of underground water, kid. It drives me into a panic. I could blow the gaff if we hit it."

"Nonsense, Mike," she said indignantly. "I know you. You can do anything you set your mind to do. You talk about luck. Most of the breaks on Blue Grouse, Mike Kendall, you have turned to the advantage of the job yourself. Jason's darned lucky to have you as super."

CHAPTER FIFTEEN

Kendall was worried. After checking and rechecking his calculations, he had fixed the breakthrough point at 126 + 00. On this sunny spring afternoon, the heading was past 115 + 20, or less than eleven hundred feet of rock to go. And still there was neither trouble nor sign of trouble. The thing was uncanny. He knew from experience that some jobs were Jonahed, that nothing ever went right with them. Blue Grouse seemed just the opposite. Save for minor incidents, the job had gone well from the start. But by the law of averages . . .

Kendall threw down his pencil at the sound of hoof-beats. He walked to the door to find Jason Tarow and Pete Trump dismounting from their saddle horses. Tarow came up the steps, hand outstretched.

"Mike, how are you? Damnably inconvenient having the telephone line out. So as long as Pete had to come, I rode along."

Kendall shook hands with his employer and with the sheriff. He ushered them into the office.

"Fran, my dear," Tarow said, taking her hand. "It's fine to see your lovely face again. I've missed you."

"It is, I think," she said with a faint trace of acid, "only twelve miles from Juniper to Blue Grouse. Now then, why one whole month?"

He shook his head sadly. "My dear, I am remiss, more than remiss. But with the tunnel approaching completion, there are a thousand and one details I must handle personally. And with my good right hand twelve miles away, why, I don't have time for anything."

"Jason, you're full of blarney. But I almost believe you. Now if you had some evidence of this press of work..."

"Oh, I have," he said triumphantly. From his inner pocket he drew a packet of papers. "I must go over these with you." He hitched his chair closer to her desk. "Fran, remember that Hepperdeizel matter? The Wishbone claim? Well, here's something new..."

As Tarow and the girl talked business, Kendall and Trump went out on the porch and sat down on the stoop. The sheriff picked up a stick and began whittling on it with a razor-keen pocketknife.

"Got your message, Mike," Trump said casually. "Looks like it's open and shut, but I had to come out and go through the motions. How's Eddie taking it?"

"Well enough. It's tough on a kid, Pete. But his uncle had turned him against him, that time he brutalized him in Juniper. I have the feeling the kid wasn't just stopping Claude from blowing the slide down on us."

"Paying off that score, eh? Well, remembering the way Claude nearly killed Eddie with that blacksnake, I dunno as I blame the kid. In any case, we'll never know, will we?"

"The man might have slipped, detonated his pack himself. That was damned long range for a .22," Kendall said.

"I've seen Eddie knock a squirrel out of a tree at two hundred yards with that popgun," Trump said. "He sure stopped Claude, for which God be thanked. I got money in Blue Grouse too."

"You think this thing was Claude's idea, Pete? Or was van Zandt back of this one too?"

"I can only add two and two. The man was in jail on a serious charge. Noble McGown, the marshal, is van Zandt's man for certain. The jailer says Noble turned Claude loose with a rifle, a Bible and a jug of forty-rod. No doubt the giant come from the

Queen powderhouse. With the hate van Zandt has for the Blue Grouse tunnel, the answer seems to fit."

"The way he is bucking the tunnel, you would think van Zandt owned the earth and the waters under the earth," Kendall said. "Pete, something Claude howled at us up on the mountain—could the Winkin Jack have been blown on purpose that night?"

"Funny you asked that. I've heard a little whisper here, and another there, in the past years, that the Winkin Jack could stand looking into. But Lord, with seven hundred feet of water in the shaft, a lot of good it would do. There couldn't be anything in it anyhow. A man wouldn't harm his own brother."

"He wouldn't? Where was Claude that night?"

"Off sick, he says, holed up in Drag Kryder's cabin. Kryder said the same thing. One thing, he sure threw a conniption when he heard his brother was dead. Damn' near went crazy, singing songs, drunk as a hoot owl, spouting that garbled gospel lingo he used to concoct. Took the boy in, too, though I had the notion the kid didn't want any part of Claude."

Tarow came out of the office then. "I unloaded my woes on Fran. Now for a look at the tunnel. Want to come, Pete?"

The sheriff shook his head. "Too nice a day to spend in a hole in the ground, even a million-dollar one. And I find I ain't happy with a whole mountain between me and the clean blue sky."

Jason Tarow laughed. He and Kendall started down the steep slant of the path toward the tunnel.

On the way to the tunnel, Kendall said, "You're not the only one who has missed the telephone. How is everything in Juniper? Have you seen Ruth lately?"

Tarow gave him an odd glance. "Why, Ruth is fine. I see her quite often, having a good deal of business with Aaron. She must give a lot of care to her mother, who is ailing. I—she does not have much time for social activities."

"Why, I hear you are the best waltzer in Juniper," Kendall said.

"Um-m-m. Here we are at the tunnel, Mike."

The three-car tram reached the tunnel entrance at the same time as the two men. Missouri sat on the front car, a bulging chaw in his leathery cheek, ready, Kendall knew, to tell all about how Doc Von Bulow had cut out the fevered appendix and had it in a bottle in his office even now. He had told both Kendall and Tarow about it several times. He stopped the mule and let the men scramble aboard a car.

As the mule drew the cars into the yellow-lit depths of the tunnel, Missouri yelled over the echoing clank of the wheels, "We got water, Mike. Hit it about a hour ago."

"So I notice," Kendall said. Alongside the track a rivulet of mineral-dark water hissed at the tie ends. The flow was of greater volume than at any time since the job began. And now Kendall realized why the atmosphere of the tunnel seemed strange. The hammering chatter of the Ingersolls was silent. "Hurry it up, Missou," he said.

"Now Mike, you cain't hurry a mule. You know that," the skinner said. He flicked the mule's rump with his willow switch. The mule paid no attention.

As the tram approached the face, Kendall could hear the sound of voices, a rumble of sounds without words, but with an undertone of excitement. Missouri stopped the mule well back from the face. Kendall and Tarow jumped out and hurried ahead.

The men of the crew were sopping wet, their clothes black in the electric lights. Kendall moved to one side, looking up. At the top edge of the working face, where it met the roof, a stream of water plunged out into the tunnel, a stream as thick as a man's thigh. The drill jumbo had been moved back. A temporary scaffold of plank had been raised. On the top of it stood Tom Hughes and one of the miners. They were maneuvering a jackhammer into position. Both of them were dripping with water.

Hughes called out, "Just a minute, Mike. Hold her right there, Bert." He leaned over the edge of the scaffold, looking down at Kendall. "We've got a powerful stream, Mike. Figured on drilling in behind it, building a grid of steel from side to side, then pushing in waste and cork and filler with the air lines. That ought to plug it."

"Worth a try," Kendall shouted. He stood as close as he could to the stream, peering up at it. He felt the horrible urge to run creeping along his loins. His muscles were shaking with the tension of staying in this place. Somehow, he managed to hold his ground. He stepped back along the platform.

"Let's get the jumbo and the jacklegs loaded into the car and away," he yelled. "They're too valuable to lose in case of a flood. Get those drifters loaded, men. Missou, haul 'em clear out to the entrance."

The men strained and grunted, loading the heavy machinery into the cars. When the last of it was in, Missou slapped the mule on the flank with the end of the rein. This time the mule started off at a good pace, in spite of the heavy tram. He doesn't like this place any better than I do, Kendall thought grimly.

"We're scrubbing this shift," Kendall called out above the splash of the water. "I want Tom, Steve Hradic, Eddie Lamb, and you, Irish to stay. The rest of you head for daylight. You too, Jason."

"I'm Staying," Jason Tarow said.

Kendall grabbed the little man's arm, shaking him. "Jason, you're my boss," he said savagely, "but by God, if you don't start down that track, I'll have Bert carry you. This work is dangerous, damned dangerous. You get yourself killed, and the whole tunnel stops. Now get a move on."

Tarow was livid with anger. He tried to twist away from Kendall. Then big Bert moved in.

"He's right, Mr. Tarow. Come on, let's go." He clamped onto the promoter's arm with one ham hand, and the little man started down the track beside him, willy-nilly. But he wasn't happy about it.

Kendall watched them go, the panic still tugging at him. He wished he could be taking that long walk toward the blessed light of day. But his men were watching him. He had to try to cope with this threatening stream of water. He moved back to the scaffold, and climbed up on it.

"Bad rock all around it," he said to Tom Hughes. "You think you can set up a plug?"

"Can't shoot a man for trying," Hughes said. "She's gonna be a wet damn' hole if we don't. What d'ya say, Mike?"

"Lend a hand with this jackhammer," Kendall growled.

Braced on the shaky platform, with a drop of twelve feet below them, they maneuvered the jackhammer into position, and Hughes kicked the loops of the air hose out of the way. Kendall raised the heavy tool, jammed the bit against the rock where Hughes indicated, and tripped the trigger. The pound of the steel shook him from head to foot. He leaned into it, feeling the bit cut into the rock. He turned his head away from the drenching spray.

He felt the resistance lessen as the point broke through. He cut off the air and pulled the drill out. Tom Hughes thrust a piece of steel up into the hole and it stayed. He pointed a finger at a new spot, above the spout of water. Kendall tripped the air. The drill bit hard as he leaned into it. Then something gave.

"Look out!" Tom Hughes yelled. Before Kendall could lower the jackhammer, he saw with horror that the rock around the leak was breaking up. A crack ran halfway across the face. Near the hole a chunk the size of a man's head tipped out, quivered, and dropped. A giant stream of water, under heavy pressure, drove out of the opening. Kendall had just time to throw the jackhammer from him when the water hit him in the chest. It drove him spinning off the staging. He doubled in midair, half drowned as he was. He hit hard, but someone below had cushioned his fall. He didn't wait to see who it was. He came to his feet running, running blindly, away from the ghastly pressure of the flood.

The water was up to his knees. He stumbled and fell, rolling. He came up, choking, to run again. Then behind him he heard a yell. The panic lifted a little. He came to a reluctant halt. And turned back.

He caught movement under the light. Catching onto a bent of timbering to keep erect in the current he called, "Come on, boys! Let's get to hell out of here!"

Steve Hradic and Tom Hughes came shuffling out of the spray, holding onto each other.

"You all right, Tom?" Kendall shouted.

"Sprained an arm, I think. But I'll make it, God willing."

He watched them go. Then Eddie Lamb and Murfree came out of the murk. He felt relief flood through him.

"Tried to save the jackhammer, boss," Murfree yelled.

"The hell with it! Get going!" Kendall said. He let go of the timber and followed them, slipping and plunging in the icy water.

The two miles to the entrance seemed interminable. Once the water rose to their waists, the tugging force of it raising the overmastering fear again in Kendall. Then he remembered the one dip in the tunnel, and true enough, when they had struggled through it, the rush of water was at their thighs again. And at long last there came the welcome glare of daylight—the tunnel entrance.

In the last few feet Eddie Lamb slipped. With a muffled cry he went under the surface. Kendall lunged for him, losing his own balance. The two of them came shooting out of the entrance like corks out of a bottle. They scrambled for footing and splashed up the bank of Blue Grouse Creek.

Kendall shook his head, spraying drops of water from his wet hair. He mopped the water from his face, blinking.

"Everybody accounted for?" he asked.

"All here," Irish Murfree said. "All wetter than me mither's cat, the toime it fell in the milk pail. Wet but alive."

Tom Hughes was cradling his elbow with his other hand.

"How's the arm?" Kendall asked.

"Sore but not busted," the foreman said. "I give it a nasty crack when I tumbled off that scaffold. Mike, did we hit the main watercourse beneath Castle Mountain?"

"We hit one dolloping mess of water, whatever it is," Kendall said. "It sure gave me a scare." He looked closely at his men, wondering if anyone had noted his shameful retreat. But they showed no sign of contempt or disgust. He breathed easier.

"If it is that water," Hughes said thoughtfully, "we're into it long before we figured it. Which means there is a real lake of it, more than anyone ever figured."

"And more than this little pinhole we punched into it will drain in a hundred years," Kendall said.

"Then we must make a bigger tap," said Jason Tarow, who had come near and stood beside them.

Kendall looked at him. The little man was draggled but still dapper. He seemed to have lost his resentment toward Kendall.

"Jason, you're right. But it is easier said than done."

Tarow shrugged. "Perhaps. But you asked for full authority, Mike. You got it. So the solution, and the next move, are yours."

"You don't have to read me a lesson in leadership, Jason," Kendall said, his anger masking the panic that still worked in him. "We'll wait until morning, just in case this is merely a pocket that can be drained. Or that the stream will rip a larger hole in that bad rock."

"But if it doesn't?" Jason Tarow persisted.

"One thing at a time, Jason," Kendall said wearily. "I'm not in shape to take on all the problems of the world at this moment. Let it go to morning." He turned to watch Eddie Lamb trotting alongside the stream. Eddie reached down and scooped some floating object from the water. He came running to Kendall, pointing at the tunnel entrance. He handed the thing to Kendall. It was an old boot, slimy with soaking.

Kendall examined it carefully and turned to Tarow.

"We were speculating on whether the tunnel had tapped the Castle Lode water," he said. "Now there's no doubt."

"That old boot, you mean?" Tarow asked doubtfully. "Why, one of the workmen might have left it in the tunnel."

"I don't think so," Kendall said quietly. "You see, this boot has the bones of a man's foot in it."

CHAPTER SIXTEEN

Pete Trump went back to Juniper, but Tarow stayed the night. The promoter was not dismayed by the insurge of water that had driven them out of the tunnel.

Not knowing the technical difficulties involved, he was enthused at the possibility that they had tapped the old workings of the Winkin Jack. When at last he let Kendall alone, and dropped off to sleep, he had exhausted all the angles, all the questions that his fertile brain could evolve. He had exhausted Kendall as well.

But dog-tired as he was, Kendall could not sleep. Again and again he came awake, his ears filled with the roar of released water. Not this minor flood of today. He was back in the Lobchick bore. The faces, blank and white, that came back to him were the faces of Plato Gill, and Raftery, and the Finn, Kollada. Men who were gone to dust on Lobchick's mountain, forgotten these years by everyone but Kendall—who could never forget.

By the time he went in to breakfast his nerves were strung as taut as banjo strings. His stomach rebelled at the thought of food. He gulped coffee, trying to thrust away the thought of that river pent in the mountain. A river, a flood, that could break into the tunnel, reaching out to drown him without a chance to escape. He set the cup on the saucer with a clash of crockery and bolted for the door. He was standing on the porch in the chill dawn wind when Jason Tarow came out.

The little man lit a long cigar and got it drawing well. "Mike, before Pete left I told him to set a twenty-four-hour watch on the

Winkin Jack shaft. The minute van Zandt hears that the water is going down—and hear it he will—he'll try to deal the project a crushing blow. I wouldn't put it past him to try to blow up the Jack."

"Why, Jason?"

"He has committed himself. Mike, you simply don't understand men like that. They are arrogant and domineering. Once they have taken a stand, no matter how untenable it is, they will go to any lengths to avoid losing face by withdrawing. Van Zandt has by now convinced himself that the success of our tunnel will ruin him. He will try to destroy us, mark my word."

"It's a damn' thin motive, though, Jason," Kendall said. He started down the steps. "But I'll let you worry about that. I've got a river to stop and a tunnel to finish. Coming?"

"You bet," Tarow said, trotting after Kendall. "Mike, I know you can lick this thing. But how will you do it?"

Kendall was silent, feeling the cold black stream tugging at his legs, at his thighs, while overhead a mountain would be poised to crumble in on top of him. He had faced it at the Lobchick. He had faced it here. No man should have to go through that a third time. He felt his joints turning to jelly at the thought.

"We'll see when we get to the adit," he said quickly, and strode ahead of the little man to avoid further conversation.

At the bridge in front of the tunnel, Tom Hughes met him.

"We drove in some marker stakes last night, Mike," the foreman said. "I just looked at them. The flow hasn't changed a particle."

Kendall nodded curtly. He stood staring at the swift flow from the mouth of the tunnel. It was, he saw, not nearly as heavy as he had been picturing in his imagination. It could sweep a man from his feet, drown him perchance. But it would never, in months or years, drain the Castle Lode. So they had to finish the tunnel.

He looked around at his men, sifting them in his mind. Hughes, grizzled and capable, with five kids and a sick wife.

Steve Hradic, loyal, able, the support of a large family. Bentz—Bert Tolan—Tod Skiffen—one by one he discarded them. At the end there was only Murfree, devil-may-care and unattached, Eddie Lamb, standing now quiet but eager, and himself, Mike Kendall. He drew a deep breath. He motioned the two men to come with him.

"You can't plug 'er, Mike," Tom Hughes said.

Kendall shook his head. "Not a chance," he said. "Jason, you tell them why we're digging this tunnel."

Tarow, surprised, said, "Why, for only one reason. To drain the water from the Castle Lode, especially the workings of the Case Ace and the Winkin Jack."

"Then we won't try to plug her. We'll run enough giant into the far end to bust 'er wide open. We already know that somehow our tunnel connects with the Winkin Jack."

"Bedad, that's the answer," Irish Murfree exclaimed. "But what brave souls are going two miles into yon mountain to do the disprit job?"

"You, for one," Kendall said with a grim smile. "Eddie Lamb, for another. And me."

"Why, I ain't sure I care for your choice, me boy. But I was niver a one to be left out of things. Let's get our tools and our necessities and blow the guts out of the whole damn' mountain!"

Eddie Lamb nodded a vigorous assent. There was a chorus of reproach from the men who were not named, but Kendall thought he could detect a note of relief even in the protests. He didn't blame them. He would mortgage his soul if he could, to get out of this task.

He sent men to bring dynamite from the magazine. He set others to building up the sides of an ore car to hold a bulky load. He had Hradic make up an explosive charge of capped dynamite sticks using the electric exploders. The whole was wrapped in oiled silk, with the bunch of wires protruding.

Tarow was almost hopping in his excitement. "Mike, tell me one thing," he pleaded, "just one thing. Your calculations show you eight hundred feet short of the Winkin Jack or the Case Ace workings. Did you make a mistake?"

"I think not, Jason," Kendall said. "I would guess this mountain of yours is a honeycomb of passages and voids. They must interconnect. If we blow a hole big enough, the whole shooting match will drain down into the Blue Grouse Tunnel."

"Mike, if it fails, if we don't drain the lode, we've ruined the tunnel. We're all through," Tarow said sadly.

"Don't you think I know it?" Kendall replied almost curtly.

Tod Skiffen was helping Hradic tie the explosive charge.

"Mike, how will you set this off?" he asked. "I wouldn't trust a blasting machine for a minute in all that wet."

"Nor would I," Kendall told him. "But the main lighting circuit?"

Skiffen rubbed his chin. Then he nodded. "Why, I guess. You hook up these caps in series, the series in multiple." He got a coil of wire and in a few minutes had the bomb properly wired. He twisted each wire end onto a heavy spring clip. "Just pinch one of these on each side of the circuit," he instructed. "She's ready to blow. But Mike, you fool around that live circuit in there, you'll be fried."

"Suppose you pull the switch out here? And leave it off until I come out of the tunnel to close it myself?"

"Sure, that would work. But if somebody closed it..."

"Knock their brains out if they come within ten feet of the switch post," Kendall said grimly. Tod Skiffen replied, "I get you, boss." He checked his watch with Kendall's, and they agreed on the proper moment for the power cutoff.

Of a sudden, everything was ready. The mine car, with its terrible cargo, with the detonator bomb deep in its center, was pushed toward the tunnel entrance. Kendall adjusted the protruding primer wires, tightened their cover of oiled silk. He stood there a long minute, staring at the tunnel. Finally he turned, his throat so dry with fear he could hardly speak.

"All right, Eddie, Irish. You ready to mule this car two miles into the mountain?"

Eddie Lamb nodded, and put a shoulder against the car. He was smiling. Kendall felt an overwhelming shame. This boy had lost his father to the flood waters, he had been through a night of horror worse than Kendall's, yet he showed no fear. So with his heart racing with panic, with his legs hurting in the urge to run, Kendall tossed away his jacket and stood in his shirt sleeves in the chill breeze. He checked his carbide lamp, and stuck pliers into his hip pocket.

"All right, boys, let's go," he said. Willing hands helped them thrust the car against the current into the tunnel. Then the three of them were alone.

In that first few yards Kendall thought he wouldn't be able to make it. The roof of the tunnel pressed down on him, the inky water hissed terror at him, the dynamite seemed on the verge of blowing up at any moment. With every step into the mountain his panic increased. Kendall clung to the car to keep from turning tail and running for the distant patch of daylight behind them.

The breaking point came and passed a dozen times. Then Kendall gasped, "Wait a minute, boys." The other two straightened up, looking at him wonderingly, their faces pale and solemn in the yellow light of the electric bulbs. Kendall turned his back. He retched until he thought his stomach would be tom apart.

When the paroxysms subsided, Kendall turned and put his shoulder to the car. He felt no better, but he had himself under control. He offered no explanation, shoving harder, keeping the car moving. They had been struggling against the water for hours, now. He sneaked a look at his watch when they reached the next lamp. Only twenty minutes? He shook the watch and found it was running.

The nightmare went on. The tunnel was interminable, the time was endless. The ghastly chill of the water crept up his thighs. His body ached with effort, but he found that in the misery of this dull torture, the panic had faded. They passed a marker, and he knew they were halfway. In one hour Skiffen would cut off the lighting circuit.

Kendall forced himself to think of the task ahead. And in thinking he found the deadly fear receding farther into the back of his mind. He was still afraid. But he was his own master again. He turned the problem of the blast over and over, figuring exactly what to do.

The slowing of the car brought him out of his preoccupation. He pushed harder. Then he felt Murfree's hand on his shoulder. He looked up, seeing the Irishman's face tired and weary in the wan light.

"Slow down, boss," Murfree said, essaying a grin. "We're at the end of the tunnel."

He had to yell above the roar of the downspout of water, pouring from the hole in the rock well above them. Kendall was astonished that he hadn't heard it before. He looked at it, waiting for the fear to drive in on him again. Instead he felt nothing, not even when he saw a large hanging slab that gave the impression of moving in the stream. Maybe, he thought, a man gets to the point where he can't bear any more. And he just quits being scared.

"We want this shot clear at the end," he shouted. They hit the car together, drove it through the column of water, into the pocket at the end of the drift. Drenched by the spray, they loosened the tarp at one side of the car, got the packet of wire ends free. Murfree blocked the car wheels with stones. Unreeling the wire, Kendall ducked back through the water into the circle of light at the last socket. He glanced at his watch. Two minutes.

"Light your lamps, boys," Kendall said. It was safe enough, with the waterfall between them and the dynamite. They snapped the spark wheels and the tiny flames blazed white. A moment later the electrics overhead blinked out.

Murfree and Eddie Lamb leaned close. In the acetylene flame, he unwrapped the scraped ends of the wires. Climbing up with the aid of a timber set, he twisted one wire end around each of the circuit wires along the roof. He crimped them hard with the pliers, and dropped back into the water. He got the tape from Eddie Lamb, climbed back and wrapped his splices first with varnished cambric, then with electrician's tape. Murfree was doing the same for the exploder ends. In seconds they were done. Kendall splashed into the water.

"Let's get out of here, boys," he panted. "I'm not happy around this much primed giant." He gave each of them a slap on the rump as they went past him.

He did not hurry. He found himself calm now, as if all the fear had burned out of him. He paused deliberately in this place of deadly danger to get his own carbide lamp lighted. No man, he thought, was ever as rotten scared as I was a while ago. I don't know what changed it. But I do know that nothing in heaven or hell will ever be able to scare me that badly again. He set the lighted lamp in the bracket on his cap. Then he turned and spat deliberately at the pounding stream of water. Only then did he set off after Eddie Lamb and Irish Murfree.

It was a long two miles. The three of them were staggering with weariness long before they could see daylight. Once Eddie Lamb went down. Kendall and the Irishman grabbed him and pulled him to his feet, sputtering and coughing. They got his lamp going again and started on. Kendall was breathing easier now, the panic behind him. But there was a permanent cold spot between his shoulder blades at the knowledge of the cracked roof slab, of the massive charge of dynamite ready to let the underground river loose on them ....

Winking toward them came a group of small white flames, the cap lamps of his men. When they met, Kendall saw it was

Hradic, and Tom Hughes, and someone who touched him very much, Jason Tarow. The little man was wet and cold and miserable, but the joy on his face at the sight of the three men was heart-warming.

"What's the matter with you idiots?" Kendall yelled. "Bad enough if the mountain got the three of us, without you men horning in."

"Was it bad, Mike?" Jason Tarow asked, as if he could guess something of the hell that Kendall had gone through.

"Bad enough," Kendall said, taking his arm, "but it's all right now. Let's get out of here."

The light of the spring sunshine was blinding. Kendall blinked the dazzling halos out of his eyes. The waiting miners gave a cheer at the sight of them. Fran Diamond ran forward, a smile on her face. Without speaking she gave one hand to Tarow, one to Kendall. Together they came up out of the wet onto the higher ground.

"Get in the clear, boys," Kendall yelled. "I want to make the shot right away. Tod, are you ready?"

Skiffen nodded, at his station beside the tall post from which the insulated wires ran into the tunnel. He still held the peavey handle ready if anyone intruded close to the live switch.

"Here's hoping," he said. "A misfire would be bad."

"You're not joshing," Kendall said. "All right, Jason. You want to blow 'er?"

Tarow looked at Fran Diamond. "We need the luck of a lady's hand. Fran, my dear, will you do the honors?"

The girl, her face flushed, walked up to the post. Gingerly she touched the wooden handle of the knife switch, its copper blades glinting in the sun. She took a deep breath. Then she thrust the switch home.

The success of this blast meant more to Kendall, probably, than anyone there. Yet he had to chuckle at the disappointment on the girl's face when nothing happened. She had expected, he guessed, that the mountain would blow sky-high. Or something equally as spectacular.

He was counting under his breath. Seconds later, he felt a slight tremor under the soles of his boots. The miners knew the score, and they gave a cheer. Then everyone concentrated their gaze on the mouth of the tunnel.

Wind whistled. A vortex of rock chips and dust blew from the opening, then a cloud of spray and muck. Momentarily, the water flow ceased. Then it began again, no heavier than before.

Tarow had his watch in his hand. "If you opened the seam, Mike, the flow would be about twelve miles an hour. Two miles, ten minutes. We'll know soon." Head down, the promoter paced back and forth. The minutes fled. Tarow's chill calm broke. "Dammit, Mike, every cent I own in the world is tied up in this thing. Yet you stand there as calm as a cigar-store Indian. You're too smug to suit me."

"Remember who pushed that ton of giant into that hole," Kendall said, not offended. "And if the shot failed, we have some other things to try. Don't give up so easy, Jason."

"He's right, Jason," Fran said soothingly. "Don't worry so much."

CHAPTER SEVENTEEN

Seven minutes—eight minutes—the tension was almost too much to bear. Then they heard a low rumble, so menacing that the onlookers drew back from the tunnel mouth. The slug of water came driving out of the bore with monstrous speed. It caught three ore cars and hurled them end over end clear across the creek. It scoured the rock in front of the tunnel, it swept boulders and debris across the creek and gouged a scar into the far bank. Its roar was deafening.

Kendall was awed by the destructive force of the flood. What have we tapped? he wondered, some kind of huge reservoir?

Tarow pounded him on the back. "It's the Castle Lode drainage, Mike. I can tell by the color. I've got to get to Juniper right away. Mike, we've won."

"Hope so," Kendall said. "But there's a lot of cleanup work to do. And Jason, remember the threats of van Zandt. That blockhead hasn't given up, I'll wager. He's liable to get mighty rough yet."

"I'm not afraid of van Zandt. With the tunnel an accomplished fact, he'll bow to the inevitable," Tarow said. "Come, Mike, I want to talk to you about dismantling the job."

Kendall shook his head ruefully. "Jason, you beat me. One minute, you're a ruined man. The next, you jump the starting line with the assurance the job is all over. Can't we wait a few days?"

Tarow tapped him on the arm. "If, tomorrow night, Aaron Hagen's steam pumps are still running, I lose. But they won't be."

"I hope you're right," Kendall said. They started up the steep path to camp, Fran Diamond just behind them. Tarow, the born organizer, proceeded to outline, step by step, the plan for closing down the job and salvaging the machinery. Kendall listened, only half hearing the little man. The reaction was setting in, and he felt ready to drop in his tracks. Beyond that, he had finished and closed out more than one hard-rock job. He knew the ropes better than Tarow did.

At the office, Tarow talked on for another half hour before he mounted his horse and rode breakneck toward Juniper. Kendall sighed thankfully as he went behind the curtain into his own quarters. He stripped off his wet clothes, put on clean drawers and trousers. Shirtless, he scrubbed his face and upper body with water and yellow soap. As he dried himself he yawned and yawned again.

He found the bottle of bourbon in the medicine chest and took a healthy slug. He took a second one to chase it and corked the bottle. The subtle warmth seeped into him. He sat down on the edge of his cot, then stretched out full length. There were things he should be doing, but...

His fitful sleep was overcharged with sketchy dreams of Lobchick and the Blue Grouse, his brother Morley, Plato Gill, Eddie Lamb, a towering giant who was van Zandt, and more pleasantly, Ruth Hagen, and recurring over and over, Fran Diamond.

She spoke out of the dream. "Mike! Mike! Wake up!"

He twisted up out of sleep, his body wet and sticky with sweat. She was sitting on the edge of the bed, smiling at him. Remembering his naked torso, he reached frantically for shirt or jacket. Fran laughed, put a palm on his bare chest, and thrust him back.

"Lie still, Mike," she said. "I was raised with three brothers. A man's bare hide is nothing new to me." She went to the table and brought a covered tray, placing it on the stand beside him.

She took the white cloth from it, revealing cold meats, bread, a pitcher of milk, a huge slab of chocolate cake.

Suddenly he was ravenous. He tackled the lunch as if he hadn't eaten for weeks. His mouth full, he said, "How'd you know I was hungry?"

She laughed. "I told you, I was raised with three brothers. And it's been a long time since breakfast."

He drank another glass of milk. "And damned little there was of that, as I remember. It seems like days ago, now."

"How come you didn't eat?" she asked.

He looked at her. "You want the truth, Fran? I was scared spitless of going into that half-flooded tunnel. My stomach was turning flip-flops from then until the blast went off."

"You mean that?" she asked, her eyes narrowed.

He nodded. "I'm a yellow dog when it comes to underground water. Ask Irish some day what happened in the bore."

"Mike Kendall, I'm happy to hear that. Why, it means that Iron Mike actually has a crack in his armor. There is something that he is afraid of."

"Many things, Fran," he reproved gently. "Have I given you the impression of being the Great I Am?"

"Not exactly. But you have worked like a model machine for the past eight months. Why, that Christmas night—" she colored a little "—was the only time you showed any human weakness."

"Hard-rock work takes hard men, Fran," he told her. "And it leaves little time for pursuing the boss's fiancée." He put his empty glass on the tray and got up. He got a shirt from the dresser and started putting it on.

It was her turn to be angry. "I deserved that," she said slowly. "Forgive the ragging, Mike." She walked to the window, came back. The smile was back on her face.

"Jason is going to close the job down as fast as he can," she said. "What do you intend to do?"

"Look for the next big job. Take a few of the best of these boys with me. I don't think the Russian thing is panning out so well, from Morley's letters. He may be back in the fall. We'll hook onto something."

"So you'll leave Juniper? And go back to playing second fiddle to your brother?"

He shrugged. "It's good enough. One shacktown is like another, one chunk of rock very similar to the last one, or the next."

"But Mike," she protested, "Blue Grouse has proved you can do things on your own, big things. Are you going to be a boomer all your life?"

"Why should I settle down? I'm a construction stiff, I don't know anything else. No girl wants to follow camp life, to endure that kind of hardship for a scarred old tomcat like me. Not that I know of, anyhow."

"Perhaps—Ruth Hagen?"

"She's a fine girl. But she'd laugh in my face."

"Mike, you know rock and powder and machinery, but it's d-darned little you know about girls! Lady or not, if Ruth Hagen finds the man she wants, she'll follow him anywhere, to the moon if necessary, and never regret it."

She picked up the empty tray and stalked out of the room. Kendall scratched his head, watching her go, wondering if he had truly seen the glint of tears in her eyes. And if he had, what had caused them? He grunted, let his creaking body sag back onto the cot, and in two minutes was asleep.

Two days later, he and Fran paid off more than two-thirds of the crew. Each man got a bonus of a week's wages, a shake of the hand, and a ride to Juniper in the company wagons. He watched the last wagon roll away in the warmth of the May sun.

"A fine crew," he said to Fran.

She made a final check on her payroll sheet. She tucked the pencil into her hair, and nodded. "Remember, you weeded them out of three times that number. And now what will happen to them?"

"Why, most of them will go into Juniper, latch onto a jug of white mule, and have a three-day drunk. They'll buy some new duds, be entertained by a fancy lady or two, and sick and broke, land on the seat of their new pants on the cobblestones of River Street. Then for them it's all to do over again."

"It's downright cruel, Mike," she said indignantly.

"They enjoy it. It's the life of a boomer. That's the way I've lived for quite a few years."

"Then it's about time you reformed," she said.

Kendall laughed and held the screen door for her.

Tarow had urged the repair of the telephone line, which gave Kendall a chance to keep Tod Skiffen and Bentz on a few days longer. And with the reports on water flow, and instructions on disposal of the machinery, Tarow would keep the line busy. The men were making only a rough-and-ready repair of the ripped-out section, but it would serve.

There was no doubt now of the success of the tunnel. The great stream continued to flow unabated from the tunnel mouth. Word from Juniper was that the water was dropping rapidly in the Case Ace, and that Tarow hoped to be able to inspect the upper levels of the Winkin Jack soon. Tarow, in his note, seemed amused at the furor and threats issuing from Phil van Zandt. "What's done is done." Tarow wrote, "and Phil might as well make up his mind to accept it. He'll thank us for the tunnel some day. But right now he's like a bear with a sore tail."

Kendall, thinking of the letter, speculated a little on how a man could become the victim of a fixed idea, as van Zandt had, to the exclusion of all logic and common sense. Then he smiled ruefully—was this worse than his own inordinate fear of water below ground? He went back to his job of calculating yardage and costs, and excavation per man-day and per ton of powder.

This final report would be valuable to Tarow. But it was the real stock in trade of a hard-rock man.

The telephone tinkled. Fran Diamond looked up from her ledger. Kendall went to the wall and picked up the receiver. The voice of Tod Skiffen was tinny with distance and his portable telephone.

"Trouble heading your way, Mike. We spotted this gang from the hill and ducked—they're past now. A dozen men on horseback, every man jack of them carrying rifle or shotgun."

"Who might they be, Tod?" Kendall asked.

"That's easy. Van Zandt was in the lead on that blazefaced black of his. I recognized that big hulk. Drag Kryder, and the tinhorn, Napper Fegg. There was a skinny dude that was likely Sprague Laurens. The rest was hardcases out of the Queen o' Hearts, I betcha."

"Most like," Kendall said. He was thinking fast. It looked as if he and Tarow had discounted van Zandt's viciousness and determination too much. And a determined man could still destroy the Blue Grouse tunnel.

"If it's safe. Tod, cut across the slide and hook onto the town end of the line," he said. "Jason's gone to Helena, but have Lock Graney rouse out Pete Trump. Tell him to get a posse over here on the double or somebody will get killed."

He did not wait for Skiffen to reply. He slammed up the receiver and ran into his room. He grabbed his rifle and all the shells he had, something over a full box, stuffed them into a jacket pocket. On the dead run he was out of the door and heading down the path.

Fran Diamond, panting, came running from her own cabin to join him. She was carrying her .410 gauge, and a large handbag that sagged with the weight of spare shells. They hurried toward the boilerhouse.

"What—what will he do, Mike?" the girl cried.

"We've got—a hell of a jag of dynamite—up there in the magazine," he told her. "He could blow in—the whole side of the mountain."

"We could set it off ourselves," she said.

"Too dangerous unless we planned for it," he said.

They burst into the boilerhouse. Kendall pulled the whistle cord six times, the emergency signal. He paused a minute, blew six more. From all around the site men came running, the canyon, the stables, the spoil pile. Down the path came Cookee, his precious knives stuck around his ample belt. Kendall breathed a prayer that the man would not fall down with all that cutlery pinned to his potbelly. Kendall counted as they came. As they waited for the last man, he noted with surprise that the stream from the tunnel, for the first time since the blast, had slacked off. It was running out now, rather than driving out. But he had no time to speculate on it. The last of the small crew had arrived.

"What's up, Mike?" Tom Hughes asked.

Quickly Kendall gave them the gist of Skiffen's message. "There's no doubt he means business," he added. "And we're in no shape to stage a gun battle."

"I got a .32 up at camp," one man volunteered.

"Yeah, with the firing pin gone," another jeered.

"Then this is all the artillery in camp," Kendall said. So boys. I want you to take to the hills. You can go up creek to Perley Fahnestock's place, beyond the falls. From there you can cut over the mountain to Juniper, and safety. I don't want the death of any man on my conscience. Get going, now."

The men looked around at each other uncertainly.

"Damn it, I mean it!" Kendall exploded. "You want van Zandt to shoot your heads off while you stand here making up your minds?"

Irish Murfree jumped up on a timber, waving his arms. "The man's right, boys. For one, I don't intend to get meself ventilated by any crazy Dutchman. Come along, now. I know the way."

When the last of the crew disappeared around the bend, Tom Hughes, Hradic and Eddie Lamb still stood stubbornly in the flat. Then Hradic said something to Hughes and the two went pelting up the hill back of the boilerhouse, with the boy trailing them. Fran Diamond watched them go, her shotgun cradled in her arms.

She looked at Kendall. "Our move, I guess," she said.

"Go on with the men, Fran," Kendall ordered. "This place won't be safe in a few minutes."

"Not me. I'm not going anywhere. You said help was coming from Juniper. You're not going to play the lone hero, mister."

Kendall had learned things that long winter. One of them was that this Diamond girl could not be budged if she had made up her mind that she was right. He looked at her now. seeing the determined set of her lovely face. She looked like a huntress, her skin lightly touched with bronze, her cropped hair a cap around her head. Her slim body had the same graceful poised strength as her face. For just a moment he tried to imagine Ruth Hagen in this tight spot. But it wasn't fair, so he dismissed the thought.

Rocks rattled on the trail above the boilerhouse. Kendall's rifle came up, then he lowered it. Eddie Lamb slid down, a coil of fuse around his neck, his hands clutching the metal boxes of blasting caps. Steve Hradic and Tom Hughes both packed a case of dynamite under each arm. Kendall sucked in his breath. If one of them had fallen, all three would have gone up in a gout of flame. But they made it, down to the boilerhouse.

"Fight fire wit' fire, see, boss?" Steve Hradic said, grinning. He ripped boards from a case and pulled the waxy sticks from their packing. Eddie Lamb unrolled fuse from a coil. He jabbed Hradic.

The boss powderman squinted one eye speculatively. He pantomimed the motions of lighting, counting, and throwing. He measured off a piece of fuse in handspans, laying a gnarled finger across it. Eddie cut the fuse to length. He took a copper cap from the box, slipped it onto the fuse end, and crimped it tight with his teeth. He handed fuse and cap to Hradic. The powderman punched a slanting hole into a stick of dynamite with a wooden fid and thumbed the cap into the hole. With cord he bound the fuse to the cylinder and put the makeshift bomb to one side. He held his hand out to Eddie for another fuse.

"After we got this powder, we triple-locked the door of the magazine," Tom Hughes told Kendall. "Mebbe it won't keep van Zandt's men out, but they'll sure as all hell be careful how they bust it open. Might delay 'em awhile. Hey, here's that Irish bog trotter back."

Murfree came down the canyon trail and joined them.

" 'Twas too much to ask a Kerryman, Mike, to keep out of what has the makin's of a lovely brawl. So once I had the boys headed right, at the waterfall, I told 'em I had to come back for me pipe. And bedad, dom if it ain't right here!" From a stump he picked up a blackened dudeen and stuck it triumphantly in his mouth.

The Irishman's return pleased Kendall, though he said, "You'll have no one but yourself to blame, Irish, if you get daylight let through you. All right, boys, that gang ought to be here any minute now. We'll see if we can hold them awhile. But the whole tunnel isn't as important as the life of one of you. So let's not take any unnecessary chances. I think we'll play it this way...."

With a stick he scratched a diagram of his strategy in the dust.

CHAPTER EIGHTEEN

Kendall sent Hughes, Hradic, and Eddie Lamb to the slopes above the boilerhouse. He was skeptical of the effectiveness of the homemade bombs, so he ordered them to retreat above the boilerhouse if they came under heavy fire. After scanning the empty hillside a final time, he followed Murfree and Fran into the boilerhouse.

Murfree was uncoiling a length of black steam hose.

"Me mother broke up many a Donnybrook with a kettle of staymin' wather," he said, coupling the hose to the hot boiler. "If these haythens get close enough I'll do as much for them."

"Good enough," Kendall said. "Fran, if they start shooting at the building, get behind the machinery."

She stuck out the tip of her tongue at him, found a vantage point along the wall of the building facing the trail, and knocked the glass out of a pane with the butt of her shotgun. She rested the barrels of the gun in the opening and waited, ignoring Kendall.

He shook his head resignedly. He looked around the long room, making sure that the rear door was open, their escape route to the canyon trail when it got too hot, as he was sure it would. He followed Fran's example and settled down to wait.

It seemed ominously quiet. Even the bird noises were hushed. Kendall could hear the soft roar of the boiler fire, the crack and snap of hot metal, the dry hiss of a steam leak. Then it came to him that the thunder of water had ceased. He found a window from which he could see the tunnel and looked out.

There was a black mark on the rock and the channel where the water had been only a few minutes ago. But the stream issuing from the tunnel was down to the size it had been just before the final blast. Blue Grouse, Kendall knew exultantly, was a success. He had drained the Castle Lode. No matter what van Zandt and his men did, Kendall had won his own battle. There was an immense satisfaction in that. He knew that never again would he feel like a small boy in the presence of Big Morley Kendall. He was, by God, a hard-rock man in his own right.

"Here come the spalpeens!" Irish Murfree shouted.

Kendall hurried back to his post. He levered a cartridge into the chamber of the rifle. Behind him he heard a valve spinning open, and the hiss of steam as Murfree charged his hose line. On the hillside Kendall spotted three men, easing their way toward the canyon, trying to take advantage of the sparse cover. He raised the rifle.

Before he could fire his warning shot, smoke geysered from the slope below the attackers. Kendall felt the jar of the explosion, heard rock chips rattle on the roof of the boilerhouse. Another bomb hammered dust into the air. The attackers scuttled back up the hill, firing wildly at the near hillside. From the rim of Bunkhouse Flat heavy firing covered their retreat. As the three dove into the safety of the brush ahead of the slam of another bomb, Kendall heard the booming laughter of Steve Hradic above him.

The firing died down. There was a long silence. Kendall watched, expecting some kind of signal for a parley. He had hoped for it, a chance for further delay, more time for Pete Trump and his posse. But it did not come. Van Zandt must be too deeply committed.

The silence was broken wide open by the crash of rifle fire. Guns opened up along the rim of the flat clear up to the point where it met the canyon wall. Accurate fire now, and heavy. Lead chunked into the walls of the boilerhouse, ripped at the roof.

Glass tinkled as a pane smashed. But much of the fire, he saw, was directed at the hillside above. Bitterly he realized his mistake. He should have concentrated his forces around the powder-house. Van Zandt couldn't do more than superficial damage without the dynamite. Still, with only two guns, could Kendall's people have defended the magazine long?

Glass crashed again. He saw Fran Diamond flinch.

"Scared, kid?" he asked.

"Darned right I am," she said tersely. "But mad, too. Wait until somebody gets in range of this scattergun."

"I'll leave him for you," he promised, and fired two quick shots at the hillside. A man had grown careless. Now he dove for the brush like a rabbit into a hole. Fran chuckled. Kendall looked over at her admiringly.

There had been no explosions for some time now. Suddenly brush and dirt erupted clear up on the rim. More than a single stick of giant, Kendall guessed. Out of the debris of the blast a man came spinning down the hill, his clothes tatters. He flopped over a bank and lay unmoving, his arms flung over his head. Kendall was surprised to feel a fierce exultation. He snapped a shot at a movement in the brush, hoping he hit the man. Any qualms he felt before were gone. This was war.

The gunfire turned now on the hill back of the boilerhouse. Kendall returned the fire, hoping to draw it from his men above.

"Whistle them in," he called to Murfree. "It's getting too rough up there."

Murfree pulled the whistle cord, sending three short blasts echoing up the canyon. Right on the echo of the last one, a heavy explosion jarred the mountainside, this time above the boilerhouse, on the near side of the coulee. Kendall jerked the door open and ran outside. He peered up at the slope, seeing only the pluming drift of dust, the flutter of movement.

"Mike, you idiot, come back here!" Fran cried. But he did not budge until he was sure he could do nothing for his men. Only then did he run for the door, bullets snapping past his head and chunking into the log walls. He slammed the door.

He picked up his rifle. "Something's happened to the boys," he said grimly. "I'm going up that hill ..."

"Here they come!" Irish yelled. Kendall whirled, rifle ready, but he saw the Irishman pointing at the rear door. In staggered the three men, sweat-stained, daubed with dirt and leaf mold. Hradic's shirt was half ripped from his body, and blood from a gash on his forehead smeared his face and dripped crimson on his singlet. With a cry, Fran Diamond hurried to him.

"He's all right, Miss Fran," Tom Hughes said. "He ain't hurted bad. Though it was a damn' near thing."

Fran was cleaning up the cut with her handkerchief and a pail of water. Hradic grinned foolishly at the attention.

"What happened, Tom?" Kendall asked, turning back to guard the trail. He saw movement and fired.

"We couldn't throw far enough after they drove us up into the timber," the foreman explained. "So we rigged a catapult, kinda like a kid's slingshot, out of two young pine trees and my jacket. First time it worked slick, we dropped a big charge right amongst 'em. But the next one hung up. We dam' near got blowed to Kingdom Come, we dropped over the edge of the bank just in time. At that Steve got the edge of the blast, and a piece of flying gravel. We seen the jig was up, so we came in."

"Good men, all of you," Kendall said. He fired rapidly, emptying the magazine. He reloaded and fired again. "It's no use, Tom, we've got to get out of here," he said.

"And the girl? No chance to surrender, I suppose?"

Kendall shook his head. "The six of us would go into some old prospect hole and van Zandt would blow it in. No, we can still get up the canyon. Fight a rearguard action if we have to. Pass the word along."

Van Zandt's men had edged closer. The firing was heavier. Kendall emptied the magazine again, the hammer clicking on an empty chamber. He thumbed shells into the loading gate, appalled at how few were left. Just then glass crashed on the far side of the boilerhouse. A bullet spanged off the flywheel of the engine, leaving a bright splash of lead.

"He sent men around the hill!" Hughes cried. "The upper trail is blocked."

Fran's shotgun fired twice. He crossed the room on the run.

"I made them duck, anyhow," she said, reloading. "What now, Mike? We can't hold them off very long."

"Dammit, why doesn't Pete Trump come?" Kendall groaned.

"Maybe he isn't coming," Fran said with an odd inflection.

"Sold out? Not Pete. Oh—good Lord, why didn't I think of that before? That skunk of a Lock Graney. He's taking van Zandt's pay. He's sitting on Tod Skiffen's message and Trump doesn't know a thing about this."

He leaned the rifle against the window frame. He put the heel of his hands against his temples, trying to think, trying to assimilate this devastating loss of hope. A hundred plans ran through his mind, to be discarded instantly. Suddenly one clicked. He turned to look out the far window. He banged his fist against the logs and didn't feel the pain.

"Eddie! Tom! Grab a bunch of cap lamps out of that locker! Irish, bring a can of carbide. We're going into the tunnel," he cried.

"Against that water?" Hughes asked, looking at him as if he were daft.

"It's down to a trickle in the last hour," Kendall said. "Look for yourself."

"Van Zandt will send his men in after us," Fran said.

"Sure. But anything is better than staying here like sitting ducks. Come on. Eddie, you and Fran first. Tom and Steve, then Irish and me. Run fast and zigzag. I'll cover you."

They did not argue. Fran handed the shotgun to Eddie Lamb, and holding her skirt high in one hand, ran from the rear door,

Eddie right behind her. Kendall raked the hill with his rifle. He
heard Tom Hughes gasp, and turned to see Fran down on her
knees. But she was up in a moment and racing for the tunnel
adit. He heard rather than saw Hughes and Hradic go, hearing
the firing from the hill intensify.

"Safe!" Murfree called out with satisfaction. "Come on, boss,
time to go."

The .30-30 clicked on an empty chamber and Kendall came
out of his crouch. He ran through the back in the wake of the
Irishman, bent low, trying to ignore the snap and whine of bullets storming down on them from the hill. Just as Murfree ducked
into the relative safety of the tunnel, Kendall felt a hard blow on
his leg. He staggered, but did not go down. Then he was into the
cold wet dark of the tunnel. The others were waiting.

"Thank God," Fran Diamond breathed, her cold fingers finding his hand.

"We're still alive, anyhow. But we've got to get farther in. Van
Zandt and his men can rake the tunnel, and sooner or later a
ricochet will get one of us. Tom, light a lamp and lead the way.
One light is all we'll risk for the present."

With a zip of the spark wheel Hughes's lamp sprang into
brightness. The shadowy tube stretched before them as he turned
toward the mountain. The rock dripped with wet, the ties and
rails were twisted unevenly by the force of the water. But outside
of that the bore was in good condition.

He and Fran brought up the rear, sloshing through the mud
and slime. He turned now and then to check the entrance, growing fainter behind them. He helped Fran over a pile of fallen
rock.

"Scared, Mike?" she asked in a whisper.

She remembers what I told her, he thought. He tried to ana-
lyze his state of mind. Afraid? Yes, he was afraid of this dark wet
hole, of the chance of a cave-in, of van Zandt's bullets driving
into his back. But it was honest, natural fear, far removed from

the senseless panic that had assailed him the day of the final blast. This he could handle, this he could face up to and spit in its eye.

"In a fashion," he told her, "but within reason."

"I'm glad," she said simply. "You know, Mike, you are actually one of the bravest men I ever saw. You just won't admit it."

"To myself I do, kid. And then I try to turn tail and run when the going gets tough, and I know it's all a stupid lie."

"But that's it, Mike—you don't run. You've licked your dread of the tunnel. You've licked your fear of running a big job. And I'll bet right now you could face up to Big Morley and make him back down. You are your own man now, Mike."

"I hope so," he said dubiously. They walked on silently, with Kendall engrossed in his own thoughts.

His leg was paining him now. He stopped for a moment and reached down to feel it, finding the stout cloth ripped, the trouser leg tacky with blood. But it hadn't stopped him. He would keep going until it did.

From far behind them came a shout. It echoed down the long reach of the tunnel, wordless but menacing. Tom Hughes doused his lamp. They stood waiting in darkness so thick it was palpable, looking back at the slight gray blotch that was the entrance. It bloomed with the yellow flare of a shot. The bullet whined off somewhere, rock chips spattered.

Kendall fired twice at the distant spot of light. He lowered the gun. "All right, Tom. Let's go," he said.

At the one low spot in the tunnel, they had to wade through icy water up to their hips. On the far side Fran stopped to wring the water from her skirt, then they went on again. Once more the racket of gunfire sounded behind them, monstrous and hollow in the echoing tube of the drift. But this time the bullets were lost somewhere in the tunnel walls and none reached them.

The tunnel seemed interminable. Hughes's light went on and on. The others followed in silence, wondering, Kendall supposed, what they would find at the end of the bore. A dead end, a cul-de-sac that would mean the death of them, like trapped rabbits? Or would there be a passage to the old workings?

The bobbing light stopped. Kendall nearly stepped on the heels of the man ahead. Then he realized that this was the end of the line. The light rails of the track were twisted and bent, the stulls and caps of the timber sets were twisted and broken, the electric wires were a snarled mass of confetti. And as Tom Hughes turned his lamp toward the roof, Kendall saw that above them there was—nothing.

"A monster cavern," the foreman said, his voice booming in an immense hollowness. "A reservoir collecting the waters of the mountain for centuries, until we tapped it."

"More recent than that, Tom," Kendall said. "Most likely drained by some natural duct until the Castle mines did something that shut it off. A blast, a rockfall. Then the water began to accumulate."

"That would be it," Hughes agreed. "For the first shafts found no water. But 'tis empty now. What do we do about it?"

Even as he spoke, a muffled thunder sounded in the drift behind them, so distorted by distance and acoustics that no one could tell what had caused it. But it decided Kendall.

"Irish, break out the rest of the lamps," he ordered. "Steve, see if you can rig that broken timber so we can scale this first ledge. It seems to slope beyond that."

Old spikes in the timber made a ladder of sorts. Kendall scaled it, found footing in the slime of the easier slope above the break. Bracing himself, he leaned down.

"Fran, you're the lightest, climb up and reach me your hand."

Without hesitation the girl came scrambling up, her face pale but determined in the carbide flame. She slipped, grabbed at him, and stood erect.

He jerked a thumb toward the hollow.

"Scared, kid? Good! Then get on up there. But don't go any farther than you can see a clear path."

As she moved past him, he slapped her lightly on the bottom with the flat of his hand. She scrambled on up into the darkness.

"What do you see up there?" he called.

"A place as big as two cathedrals," her voice came hollowly down the shaft. "But no sign of daylight."

"Stay there," he shouted. "Come on, Eddie, you're next."

CHAPTER NINETEEN

As the last man climbed past him, to disappear into the darkness above, Kendall reached out a foot and kicked the timber away into the tunnel. Then he followed the others up into the cavern.

Fran was right. The void was an immense thing, glistening with slime, misshapen in places where stalactites dripped from the roof. Their puny lamps hardly penetrated its gloom, beyond some faint shadows of reflection in the black. Just in front of them was the ebon surface of a pool, the water motionless, rippled now and then by the dropping of water or debris from above.

Kendall studied it. He shifted his weight, grunting at the pain of his bad leg. Fran turned toward him, alarmed.

"Mike, what's the matter? Did you hurt yourself?"

"Van Zandt's men nicked me as I ran for the tunnel. I don't think it amounts to much," he said, impatient to be moving.

"You could bleed to death," she said severely. She borrowed a pocketknife from Murfree and slit open the trouser leg. Kendall heard her suck in her breath when she saw the wound. But her voice was matter-of-fact when she said, "Flesh wound. But I could lay a finger in the groove of it. Eddie, let me have your shirttail. My petticoat is too wet and muddy to tear up."

She bandaged the bullet slash tightly. "Try it now, Mike," she said.

He stood up, finding the support of the bandage easing his pain.

"Thanks, Fran," he said. "Well, you boys come up with anything?"

The light on Tom Hughes's cap dipped. "Taking our line from the tunnel, our course is straight across that pool. Looks as if we could skirt the edge of it. Since we know the water was draining from the Case Ace and the Jack, somewhere on the other side we should meet up with a connection to the workings of one or t'other."

"I can't think of anything better," Kendall said. He jacked the shells out of the rifle and put the precious few carefully into his pocket. With the empty gun serving as a staff, he hobbled to the edge of the pool. "All right, Eddie, I remember you can swim. You tackle it first."

Without hesitation the boy eased his way forward, Tom Hughes moving after him until Hughes was hip deep. Eddie's lamp bobbed lower, lower. He was up to his waist now, his chest. Then they heard him grunt, and quickly the lamp came higher. He climbed out on the far bank, the water cascading from his soaked clothing. He turned a triumphant face toward them and beckoned them to come.

Steve Hradic followed Hughes and Eddie across. Fran Diamond hesitated as she came to the edge of the ominous pool.

Irish Murfree grabbed her, swept her up in his arms.

"Ah, mavourneen," he cried, " 'tis the first chance I've had to cross water with a girl in me arms since I left Kerry. I'll show ye how we used to ford the little streams that ran into the Laune, when I was a boy near Cloghereen." Holding her as high as he could, he splashed into the water. At the middle her feet dipped into the water, but she did not cry out. On the far side Murfree set her down on the rock. "And our reward from the colleen, Miss Fran," Murfree said laughing, "was a kiss or a slap, dependin' on how busy our hands were in the course of the crossing!"

Kendall saw the girl go up on tiptoe, to touch the Irishman's cheek with a kiss. As he went toward them through the icy water, he found himself touched at the girl's gentle gesture. This, he thought, is a man's woman. He remembered Ruth Hagen's words, "Fran came up out of the gutters of Juniper because of what she is, through her raw courage and brains and mother wit." He could see, now, why Ruth envied these qualities in Fran, though she had her own fine character and abilities and courage.

He bumped into Murfree and came out of his reverie. Ahead Eddie Lamb had stopped and was pointing upward. They had come to a pile of slime-encrusted rock. Above it rose the abrupt face of the cavern wall. In the wall they could see the deeper blackness of a cave. Perhaps this was their escape route. Even though the pile was loose and dangerous, it had to be explored.

"Eddie, Tom, Steve—go ahead and find what we have. The three of us will wait here," he said.

They climbed up the pile, slipping in the treacherous footing as careful as they were. They reached the ledge below the opening. Their lights dimmed and disappeared as they went out of sight in the drift, leaving the cavern gloomier than ever.

"What do you think, Mike?" Fran asked tersely.

"We'll make it, kid," he told her, putting more confidence in his voice than he felt.

Long minute followed minute. Kendall was about to send Murfree after the others when a light appeared above them. It was Hughes.

"Mike, we need you up here," he called. "Not Miss Diamond, though. Better leave her with Irish." Kendall caught a peculiar intonation in the Welshman's voice.

Grunting with the pain of his sore leg, Kendall climbed up the treacherous slope, using the butt of the rifle to aid him. At the top Tom Hughes reached out a hand and swung him to the flat.

"An old drift of the Winkin Jack," Hughes explained as they went along the man-made tunnel. "Why I said not to bring the girl—well, you'll see for yourself, Mike. And you won't believe it any more than we do."

They went into the tunnel. It had been under water, coated with slime and muck like the rest of the cavern. A little way inside, Hughes stopped and pointed down. Kendall saw a bundle of rags, the white shine of clean bone, the rotten leather of a boot. A skeleton without a skull. Kendall straightened and hurried on.

Then, startlingly, the slime and wet ended. This tunnel was dry, even dusty. Their lamp flames dimmed from reduced oxygen. Kendall coughed and followed Hughes to the end of the gradually ascending drift.

Here was a room with the mine tracks still intact. In its center stood Eddie Lamb, as if frozen with horror. Along the wall, in attitudes of rest or sleep, were five men. Kendall had to come closer to discover, with a shock, that these were dead men, their bodies mummified by the still, cold air of the mine.

"Eddie's father," Hughes explained, "and the other men who were in the Jack when the water broke through. They ran in front of the flood, through drift and crosscut, to end up here, trapped. They might have gotten out, but look ...." He led Kendall over to the square darkness that was a raise. He pointed upward.

Kendall squinted in the ineffective light. Then he saw it—the raise was blocked, not by rockfall or timber, but with a solid mass of concrete. He looked at Hughes. His foreman nodded. They went back into the large room.

"They still had a chance," Hughes explained. "The whole mountain is honeycombed with shafts and stopes and raises. But I'm sure now that the first flood, the one that drove them here—" he swung an arm toward the silent men "—was due to a blast. And that wasn't all. Another blast sealed off this drift. These men sat here and died slowly as their oxygen gave out."

"Who? And why?" Kendall asked, his voice shaking.

"Frank Lamb will tell you," Tom Hughes said, pointing at the first of the five bodies. Kendall walked over to it. Eddie Lamb was kneeling beside it, his face bowed into his cupped hands. He did not move as Kendall reached down and took the stained notebook from the clawlike fingers of the mummified body. In the light of his cap lamp Kendall turned the pages, a great and selfless anger rising in him as he read.

"If anybody ever finds us," the crabbed penciling in the notebook read, "it was van Zandt done this. They was tapping our vein from their 1100, they was way over in our ground. Fegg was pushing the crew he went too far broke into our drift. We lit into them but van Zandt come with a gun drove us back. Then they blew our 1200 level and the water come in. They wouldn't let us into their workings. We come through a crosscut into this drift I knew about, old drift, I knew about a raise, went into the Queen. When we got here it was blocked with concrete. We tried another way, they blew it up in our face and the water come in again sealed us off. The air is getting had now, two days. Can't give up yet maybe somebody will break through. I am praying my boy Eddie got out of this safe I sent him on a errand to the main shaft just before Fegg come. He is just a kid don't know about all this.

"I think the Queen has hit borrasca so van Zandt is stealing Winkin Jack highgrade. I hope he will rot in Hell for what he done to 7 good men with families most of them. And Claude Lamb my own brother he was the one set off the second blast. He is a Judas, Claude I don't know how you could do that thing. You alluz raved about them fires of damnation you will burn in them Claude for what you done I hope you choke on van Zandt's gold.

"EVERYBODY TAKE NOTE PHILIP VAN ZANDT HE DONE THIS MURDER OF INNOSENT MEN HE IS THEIF LYAR AND MURDERER.

"It is hard to see the last lamp is going out I must stop my writtin I hope someboddy finds this but likely not ever but I done my dambdest and what could any man do more than that. So I say God Bless You Eddie I hope you are safe and may GOOD GOD HAVE MERCY ON THE SOULS OF US AND ALL PORE MINERS.

Frank P. Lamb
June 6 or thereabouts I think
1894"

The pity and the hate were a fire in Kendall as he closed the little book and placed it in his pocket. He lifted Eddie Lamb to his feet and put an arm around the boy's shoulders. He said the one thing that would bring the boy out of the depths of his grief.

"Eddie, van Zandt is coming. You know the mine. How do we get out of here?"

The boy raised his tear-stained face. He choked back his sobs. Angrily he wiped his shirt sleeve across his face and straightened. He took one last look at his father's body and turned away. He pointed toward an opening in the far wall. A crosscut.

Then beyond the drift they heard the slam of Fran's shotgun. Kendall forgot his game leg. He raced limping down the length of the drift. He breathed a sigh of relief as he saw two lights bobbing toward him.

"They're up out of the tunnel," Murfree panted. "Miss Fran fed them a dose of shot, that ought to delay the divils."

"Good girl, Fran," Kendall said. He doused his light and went to the tunnel end. Beyond the pool, a light gleamed for a moment. Kendall flung two quick shots at it. Then, knowing this position was untenable, he hurried back toward where the other two waited.

"I think Eddie can get us out of this," he said. "Fran, douse your light too. We may need it later." On this excuse he was able to guide her through the long room to the crosscut where the others waited, without her catching sight of the bodies. The sight would haunt him for many a month. He didn't want her to have nightmares over it.

With Eddie Lamb leading the way, they hurried down the dimness of the crosscut. They came to a junction. Eddie hesitated a moment, then raced ahead. The crosscut dipped. Once more they found the slime and muck of a once-flooded area. They went down, now on a long slant. The tunnel widened, the timbering was heavier. They broke out into a chamber, a vertical shaft thrusting up from it. The main shaft of the Winkin Jack.

More than three years since a cage had run in this shaft. But Kendall gave an audible sigh of relief.

"Eddie, you're a genius!" he said, slapping the boy on the shoulder. "We're not in any shape to stand off van Zandt's men. I've got four shells left in the .30-30. Fran's fixed better with her shotgun, but ..."

"I'm sorry, Mike," she said in embarrassment, "but remember when I tripped, running for the tunnel? I lost the box of shells. I've got one lone shell in the breech of this gun."

"Luckier still, then," Kendall said. "Come on, let's get a move on, boys."

The safety ladder went up and up into the darkness. Steve Hradic started up it, then Hughes, and Irish Mur-free. Eddie Lamb took the .410 from the girl, broke it, and hooked it through his belt. Then he started up, to disappear high above them. Mud and rock and water dribbled down, to plop into the pit. Fran Diamond drew a deep breath and started up. Kendall held her in the beam of his lamp until she was well up the shaft.

He slung the rifle over his shoulder and grabbed the rungs. His job, he knew, was to bring up the rear. The other reason he hadn't told his people was that he did not know how long the injured leg would hold up. If it crumpled, so that he fell, he would not sweep anyone else to his death. He started up the ladder.

He gritted his teeth as he took one slow step after another. His leg was laced with fire, the sweat dripped from him. In the light of the cap lamp the wall behind the ladder was green with ooze. He made fifty rungs, and rested. Fifty more.

The leg was weakening. He was taking most of his weight on his arms now. They tired, and he rested more frequently. Thirty rungs now. Then twenty. Twenty more. Ten and a rest. And the wall was dry. The discovery gave him a new lease on life. He made twenty rungs. Then of a sudden he reached up and found nothing. He stared stupidly at the bare rock of the wall. There was no more ladder.

He almost let go when a voice said in his ear, "Over here, Mike. One long step. Easy, now." He stepped over, onto dry solid rock, and went involuntarily to his knees. Murfree helped him up.

His leg was a vast throbbing pain. He ached with utter weariness. "Where are we?" he asked dully.

"Old six hundred level of the Winkin Jack," Tom Hughes said. "Van Zandt's men must have pulled the ladder as far down as they could go into the Jack. But Eddie just wrote a note that we can get from this level over to the Case Ace. They had a joint air shaft at one time. You all right, skipper?"

"I'll make it," he said grimly. He unstrapped the rifle and limped forward. Fran Diamond dropped back to help him. Eddie Lamb went ahead, Fran's shotgun under his arm.

Kendall was certain that he couldn't make another fifty yards. Yet somehow he managed it. He knew then that no matter how bad the pain got, he would still continue until all his crew were safe. He wondered if van Zandt's men were climbing that hellish ladder behind them. He was so weary he didn't much care.

Light loomed ahead. Eddie reconnoitered. He came back, shrugging. They followed him into a new drift and into the blessed light of the row of electrics strung along the roof. Kendall saw his men smiling. Freedom could not be far away. They waited for Eddie Lamb to indicate their route.

But there was a confused look on the boy's face.

"What's the matter, kid, this new to you?" Kendall asked.

The boy nodded vigorously.

"Then make your best guess," Kendall said.

Eddie Lamb hesitated, then pointed left. They followed him down the drift. Kendall limped along, wondering a little, for the tunnel was too clean, with no signs of recent activity. No matter. They would come to an exit or a miner, sooner or later.

The tunnel curved, twisted away. Suddenly it broke out into a large room, from which a pocket must have been cleaned out, for there was heavy timbering, and here or there a pillar left undisturbed. Eddie Lamb stopped, bewildered. Kendall limped ahead, looking for the incoming wires of the electric circuit.

As he reached the middle of the room, a noise brought him to a dead stop. His mouth dropped open in surprise. From the opposite opening came six men, wet, dirty, but armed. Van Zandt's men, as startled as Kendall was. Napper Fegg, Kryder, two hard-case miners. And van Zandt himself, his face twisted with anger, the strained face of a man driven by devils. Or ghosts.

Kendall's mind was racing. This drift, then, was part of the bootleg workings of the Queen o' Hearts. Fegg, van Zandt's man, would know the underground, the crosscuts and the raises. They had found a short cut through these workings, and had hurried to cut Kendall and his men off at the Winkin Jack shaft. Well, the plan had worked after a fashion.

Kendall swung his rifle up, centering it on the mine owner just above the stained cast of the broken arm.

"Stop where you are," he said harshly.

"Get him, men," van Zandt ordered.

Only Drag Kryder made a move. As his gun swung up, Kendall, without pity or hesitation, shot him through the body. The huge man dropped to his knees, then pitched forward, bouncing a little, like a grotesque clown. He groaned once and lay still.

"One, van Zandt," Kendall said.

"Five to go, all armed," van Zandt said. "What do you think you can do about it?"

"Take you to the surface and turn you over to Pete Trump. Who will hang you for murder."

"You don't know the facts of life, Kendall," the mine owner jeered. "First of all, they don't hang a million dollars in Montana. Especially when there are no witnesses—alive."

"You can produce the million?"

"And more. Oh, I've had a very nice thing here, Kendall. I don't intend to let that fool Tarow spoil it with his tunnel. I know more about this mountain than any man alive. I blocked off the Winkin Jack, and then drowned out their workings. Then I took two million dollars in picture rock out of their leads. Why, when water seeped into our workings, we turned it into the Case Ace, for Aaron Hagen to handle with his damned steam pumps!"

"Very clever, van Zandt," Kendall said, hoping to anger the man into a wrong move. "So you admit you are a thief and a killer. Well, you'll never live to enjoy your loot."

"I think so," van Zandt said. "After we dispose of you, we'll put Tarow away, then destroy the Blue Grouse tunnel. No witnesses, no indictment. The fools who live in Juniper will consider that I am their most prominent citizen. And I will be."

Kendall felt the cold edge of fear touch him. The man was ruthless, probably crazy. But the plan would work. Recklessly, he stepped forward, seeing Napper Fegg edging to one side, one of the toughs to the other. Crossfire.

"Prominent citizen, hell!" he jeered. "You're nothing but a damned filthy murderer!"

Van Zandt merely laughed. "Juniper won't think that. Why, Mr. Kendall, who am I supposed to have killed?"

From behind Kendall there came a strangled cry. Eddie Lamb stepped past him. Fran's shotgun was in his hands.

"You—van Zandt!" Eddie screamed. "You killed my father!" And he shot Philip van Zandt through the heart.

CHAPTER TWENTY

Mike Kendall was alone in his room in the Elkhorn, feeling miserable and abused. His chest was slippery with goosegrease and camphor, his mouth cloyed with horehound. He sat in a bathrobe, his bare shanks sticking out from under his nightshirt, his feet soaking in a pan of mustard water as hot as he could bear. There was a stack of clean handkerchiefs on the stand beside him. On the floor was a mound of soggy, crumpled ones. He coughed and spat and groaned. In short, Mike Kendall had the grandfather of all colds.

More than that, he was disgruntled and put upon. Doctor Von Bulow had been in briefly, to dress Kendall's leg wound and give him specifics for his coryza. The doctor had fussed around, never stopping his chatter.

"Oh, yes, that Eddie Lamb. Very nize case. I joost might write it up for the medical journals. Brain fever, you understand, gomplicated by the flooding of the mine and the death of his fadder. In Vienna dis is called a 'mental block.' Great mental stress the cause, so great mental stress the cure. Fery interesting—he sees his fadder's body, he sees van Zandt, his voice must come back so he can accuse the man."

"Is he all right now?"

"Eddie? I joost had him in my office for treatment." The doctor leaned forward, his eyes twinkling. "You know what for? The boy hass himself a sore throat—from talking too much since!" Still chuckling, he snapped his bag shut and departed.

Pete Trump had been Kendall's next visitor. "It's like a house of cards, Mike," he said. "One card out and the whole thing comes tumbling down. With van Zandt dead, all his henchmen are spilling everything they ever knew. We've got the whole story now."

"Any trouble in store for the boy, for shooting van Zandt?"

Trump shook his head. "I doubt it. We'll go through the motions of an inquest on Phil and Kryder, but there's no doubt both of you acted in self-defense."

"Van Zandt was doing as he bragged, cleaning out the lode?"

"They had been stripping the best veins for months, taking it out through the Queen, as Queen ore. It's hard to believe he could keep it hushed up, but he was a tough hombre—I know now that several of our unsolved killings can be laid to him and Kryder. I guess none of his men dared to talk."

"Where do Tarow and the Luscon Syndicate stand?"

"They may have to sue van Zandt's estate to recover, but they'll get it eventually. Or settle with Thelma van Zandt, for a price. I think she can be had. She isn't shedding any tears over Phil. She'd like to latch onto Sprague Laurens and shake the dust of Juniper off her feet, I'll wager."

"I'm still concerned about poor Eddie."

"Mike, after what was found on the 1200 level of the Winkin Jack, the town of Juniper and the State of Montana ought to award Eddie a medal. Van Zandt was a clever, ruthless devil. We'll watch out for the kid, don't you fear."

After Trump left, Kendall suffered alone. His chest hurt, his nose was sore from blowing. And the mustard water in the foot bath was growing cold. Damn it, a man could die in this firetrap without a soul lending him a hand. A fine thing, after building Blue Grouse ....

He was reaching for a fresh handkerchief when a knock came at the door. "Come in," he growled.

It was Ruth Hagen, radiant of face, beautiful in a frilly spring gown. Behind her came Jason Tarow. Ruth hurried over to Kendall, making soothing noises, placing a cool hand on his burning forehead.

"Mike, you poor boy, you're ill," she said.

"I'll get over it," he said. "Without that Dutch pill-roller, too. He gave me a handful of horse medicine, told me to keep up just what I was doing, and charged me a dollar."

"I'll wager you growled at poor Doc a dollar's worth, too," she said, smiling. "Jason, maybe your medicine will help Mike more than the doctor's."

With a flourish Jason Tarow opened his wallet and took out a slip of paper. He handed it to Kendall.

Mike Kendall looked at it. He tried to purse cracked lips to whistle. "Twenty thousand!" he exclaimed. "How come, Jason?"

"You saved us many times that, besides what we hope to recover from the van Zandt estate," the little man said. "But I have something better, Mike. I want you to stay in Juniper as the superintendent of all my operations."

Kendall rubbed his chin. "That I'll have to think over, Jason."

"Take your time." The promoter looked at Kendall, and away. He burnished the nails of his hand on his coat sleeve. Finally he looked at Kendall and said, "We have other news, Mike. Ruth and I will be married the first of next month."

The announcement startled Kendall. But it did not jolt him as he would have expected. He watched Ruth, her face illumined, move over to stand beside Tarow. Though she stood a head taller than the little man, she made no apologies. Kendall could not deny the sincerity of the girl.

"Mike, I love him—I have for a long time," she said simply. "Remember when I said Fran had something I envied? It was Jason's promise."

"And what of Fran?" he asked. "It was a promise, Ruth."

"It was, Ruth," Tarow said. "I feel like a rotten cheat in breaking it."

"A clean break is better than a living lie," Ruth said.

"Have you told her?" Kendall asked.

Tarow nodded, his face sad. "She took it well. Like the lady she is. But I know it hurt."

"Only yesterday she risked her life to help save Jason's property," Kendall reminded them. "Is this her reward?"

"Mike, I've been a nice girl, a real lady, all my life," Ruth said proudly. "Now for once, I'm going to be merciless to anything that stands in my way. My claim to him is greater than Fran's, for it is the claim of love. And I think she never loved him."

"That is a surmise, Ruth," he said.

"Just the same, I mean it. Just think of it, Mike. Daddy's holdings and the Luscon will be one unit, ready for great things."

"Sure, let's be practical, no matter who gets hurt. But take my best wishes, children. Forgive the fact that I'm grumpy from this cold, and resentful because once I was half in love with Ruth myself."

"I knew that," she said. "But it has been Jason since the first day we met five years ago. Except he didn't know it. Goodbye, Mike."

Careless of his cold, she stooped swiftly and kissed him on the cheek. Then they were gone, leaving the room strangely lonely.

Kendall had not lied when he said that once he had been half in love with Ruth. But he found that now he had no deep regrets for her decision. His concern was for Fran Diamond. The humbling of her gay pride, her humiliation at being jilted—how much would they hurt her? A great deal, he knew, for under her carefree ways he had learned that Fran was sensitive and vulnerable.

They had grown close in that year, he thought. He smiled at his introduction to the girl, in this very room, how fierce she had been in guarding Jason's interests. He shook his head at the memory of that Christmas night at Blue Grouse. What a fool he had made of himself! He remembered the rides with her, the trout fishing, the long hours of work together. And at the last, her gallant part in the desperate flight from van Zandt, with never a whimper from her. Why, that girl was a dandy. She would rate A Number One in anybody's book. When he left Juniper ...

Suddenly he was appalled. He couldn't leave her in Juniper. A man would be a fool to leave this lovely girl of the forthright way and the gallant smile. The feeling that swept over him was a wrench of pain. Was this the crazy thing called love, or was he sicker than he thought? No matter. He had to see Fran Diamond. Now.

He stood up, spilling the basin, careless of the wet tracks he made across the room, searching for his clothes. He was still in his bare feet, but dressed in shirt and trousers, when another knock came on his door. He swore softly, scuffing into slippers. Whoever it was, he'd get rid of them in short order. He opened the door.

Fran Diamond walked in. In a spring frock, her hair groomed, she was so lovely that his heart turned over. She pirouetted for him, her arms outstretched.

"Like it, Mike?" she challenged. "I had to do something. When a girl has been jilted, she must do something to save face."

He dropped into a chair, reaching for a fresh handkerchief.

"It's beautiful, Fran, and so are you. How are you taking it?"

She sat on the hassock beside him. She looked straight at him with that clear direct glance of hers.

"I won't say it didn't hurt, Mike. But after the first shock of it, I knew Ruth was right—my love for Jason was never as deep as hers. With it over, I feel oddly free."

"They are my friends, I'm fond of both of them. But they took a few chips out of that friendship when they told me what they had done to you." He blew his nose furiously, rubbed it hard.

She put a hand on his. "Don't feel that way, Mike. Jason was more of a symbol to me than a fiancé. You know, and I know, that he is destined for great things. It's in his nature, just as it's in your nature to build things. As his partner, helping him attain those great goals, I'd be climbing higher myself."

She was silent a moment. Her hand tightened on his. She went on in a soft voice, "Mike, my mother was a saloon girl at the Oxbow. My father was a charming, no-good scoundrel. This far, I've come up out of the gutters of Juniper. What I know, I taught myself. What I have, I earned myself. I was gunning for the position and the wealth that will one day go with Jason Tarow. But now I know it's no good. Ruth and Jason are perfectly suited. I say let them go their way in happiness, with all my love."

"Good girl," he said. A spasm of coughing caught him, shaking him. When it stopped he mopped tears from his eyes.

"Mike, that's an awful cold!" Fran said. "You'd better get back in bed."

He shook his head. "More important things to do," he said. "You didn't have any such ill effects from your jaunt underground?"

"I dreamed all night that Phil van Zandt was chasing me down dark tunnels, right on my heels," she said, shivering a little. "And Drag Kryder, falling like a great tree; and van Zandt, with the disbelief in his wild face when Eddie shot him." She covered her face with her hands. Finally she looked up, her face composed. "I know they deserved it, Mike. But I'd never seen a man die in sudden violence."

His hand sought hers. "You were superb, Fran. I'm proud of you."

They were silent for a long time. Then Fran stirred.

"Important things, Mike. What could they be?"

"Deposit this check in the bank. Write out my regrets to Mr. Tarow, sorry I can't take his fine position as super. But the itch is in my feet and the far hills are calling. Next, to the telegraph office to send a wire to Morley Kendall, the Astor House, New York."

"Saying what?" she asked, her face serious.

"Saying I'm taking on a bridge job for Heppelthorp & Rand north of Vancouver, asking him if he wants to take the night shift. That will burn him until he smokes. Especially since the Russian thing fell flat."

"But the rest of it is true?"

"As Gospel. Want to come along?"

She looked at him, her lovely face startled. He watched her, cursing this cold. He used his handkerchief again, irritated that this thing made him not only uncomfortable but ridiculous. How could a man propose to a girl when his nose was dripping?

"Fran, both of us grew up on the Blue Grouse job. You know that."

She nodded, not taking her eyes from him.

"We're two of a kind, a pair to draw to. On top of that, I find I'm in love with you. Just make up your mind. I'm not heading west without you. All right?"

She nodded again. Then she smiled radiantly. She came into his arms.

Minutes later he held her away from him. "Darling, get away from me. You're going to catch my cold."

She turned, her arms going around his neck.

"Who cares?" she exclaimed. "What's yours is mine...."

"Aaah-h-*cHOOH!*" sneezed Mike Kendall.

THE END

www.ingramcontent.com/pod-product-compliance
Lightning Source LLC
Chambersburg PA
CBHW022157240626
47153CB00007B/2698